Another Chance

Hidden Treasures, Broken Pieces

Another Chance

Hidden Treasures, Broken Pieces

Denise A. Smith

Inscript Books
A Division of Kingdom Christian Enterprises
PO Box 611
Bladensburg, MD 20710-0611

Paperback ISBN 978-1-957497-47-1

Printed in the United States of America

This book is dedicated to the giver of my gift, My Heavenly Father and Jesus Christ my Lord and Savior.

My God I cannot express my gratitude for creating me, pursing me, and redeeming me. This life has been difficult. But finally realizing the price that was paid for us to come into an eternity with you is worth every tear I have ever shed, every heartache I ever felt and every pain I couldn't explain. Your love is overwhelming. Your word is living water in my soul that will never allow me to thirst again. You are greater than anything I have; anyone I know and any path that doesn't lead to you.

Thank you for your patience, thank you for your grace and thank you for brand new mercies over and over again. You lovingly waited for the arrival of my soul and spirit to say yes. So, that in which you have given to me, I give it back to you. Thank you for the message you have given to me to share with the world. A reminder that your love, grace, mercy, and patience for us is beyond what we could imagine. And this type of love is not limited to a second chance but as long as we have breath in our bodies we have ANOTHER CHANCE. Glory be to the only true and living God. You are ABBA.

Proverbs 2:1-5:
My son, if thou wilt receive my words, and hide my commandments with thee; So that thou incline thine ear unto wisdom, and apply thine heart to understanding; Yea, if thou criest after knowledge, and lifetest up thy voice for understanding; If thou sleekest her as silver, and searchest for her as for hid treasures; Then shalt thou understand the fear of the Lord, and find knowledge of God.

Read the first book in this series by Denise Smith:
*Hidden Treasures Broken Pieces: Dangerous
Decisions*

Table of Contents

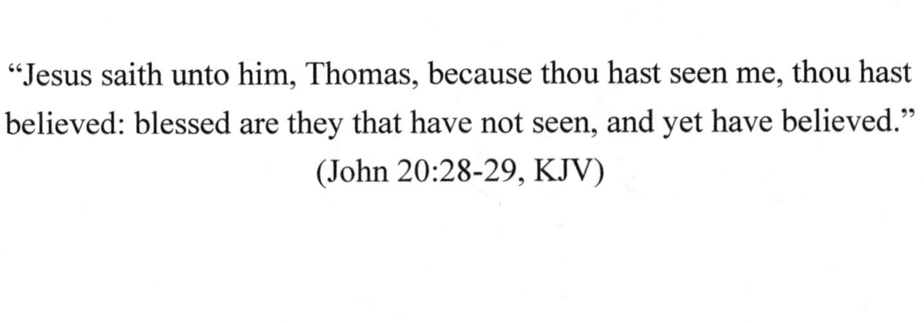

"Jesus saith unto him, Thomas, because thou hast seen me, thou hast believed: blessed are they that have not seen, and yet have believed."
(John 20:28-29, KJV)

Prologue

DeVon has been in the hospital in a coma for seven days. Jay has been by his bedside every day, praying for God to heal his boy. With his eyes closed and his hands holding DeVon's, Jay was once again begging God to save his life. His prayer was interrupted by the sound of a slight cough and the movement of DeVon's hand. He opened his eyes and couldn't believe what he saw. Running out of the room and down the hospital hallway, he yelled:

Jay: HELP, HELP, HE'S WOKE. NURSE, HE'S WOKE.

As he pulled the nurse into the room, she saw DeVon's eyes open and look around in confusion. He was unable to speak a word with the machine breathing for him. The nurse buzzed the doctor into the room, and the examinations began. As the doctor began removing all the equipment, he explained to DeVon how lucky he was.

Doctor: Young man, to say you have been through a lot is an understatement. You are what we consider to be a miracle in this hospital. Tell me how you feel.

DeVon: (*confused and looking at Jay*) In a lot of pain, doc. What happened? How did I get here?

Doctor: You were shot and crashed your car. Do you remember anything?

DeVon: No, I don't (*still confused*).

Doctor: I am going to let you gentlemen discuss the details. I need to get some blood work drawn on you and something for pain. I will notify the police that you're awake. Young man, what a miracle you are.

DeVon: (*coughing*) What is going on? What happened to me, man? (*coughing again*).

Doctor: Don't stress yourself. It's not good for your body right now. Chances are you're having short-term memory loss, which is common after tragic events.

DeVon: Jay, what's going on?

Jay: Just rest. I will tell you, but you have got to calm down. You are working yourself up. You need to get your thoughts together, and we need to thank God for your healing. You have been in a coma for seven days.

DeVon: Seven days? Why?

The nurse began to pump pain medication into DeVon's IV, and he instantly became drowsy and coherent. Because he could no longer talk, he looked at Jay and saw tears in his boy's eyes. He was still unable to make sense of it all. *Why would someone shoot me?*

Nurse: Well, that didn't take long at all. He will be out of it for a while. It's best for patients to get as much sleep as possible when going through an ordeal like this. It helps with the swelling of his brain. So let him sleep. Besides, you look like you could take a moment and go home, shower, and eat. Rest a little before coming back.

Jay: Thank you, but no thanks. He has no family (the *nurse looked confused*). Only my wife and I, and I am not leaving for him to wake up alone. My wife will come relieve me later today so that I can run home. She will sit with him while I'm gone.

Nurse: Well, he is one lucky guy to have you both *and* his fiancée.

Jay: Fiancée? What are you talking about? He is not engaged.

Nurse: (*looking confused*) The lady that sits with him when you go downstairs to the cafeteria to eat during the day. She's sweet (*with hand gestures, she gives a description*), she's about yay tall, fair skin, and just beautiful. She knows everything about him.

Jay: (*anger boiling within*) Ma'am, she is not his fiancée. She is the reason he is in this condition. If she comes in here again, you call me and the police immediately. Do you understand?

Nurse: I'm sorry, I'm confused. She said she was just sitting with him while you gathered yourself and got something to eat. It seems like as soon as you would come back, she would leave, so I figured she was nearby and was helping. The nurse on the overnight shift says she comes and sits with the two of you at night also. I will have to let the doctor know and decide.

Jay: My apologies for my behavior. You can tell whomever you need to tell. Just know if she comes back, she needs to be removed immediately, and I need to be called. Please, ma'am.

Jay couldn't believe his ears. He thought to himself, *this piece of a woman had the nerve to come to see him when she was the cause of all of this. She needs to go to jail right along with her punk piece of a man husband. If she thinks for one minute that she is going to talk DeVon out of pressing charges against this man, she is crazy.*

Jay: (*talking out loud to himself*) I know she don't think she's that good....

Chapter One

<u>Pass Me Not</u>

<u>DeVon's thoughts:</u>

Through hospital IV, fluids of anger pump through my veins. As rage fills my heart, I will never be the same. Too many blows I've taken in this life. None of them I have asked for, so you tell me why.

Why should I continue to believe in someone I can't see? Someone who has all power but didn't protect me. From birth, cursed into this world of darkness and rage. Like an animal, when I get out, he will see my face.

Justice is mine now, vengeance in my hand. The hurt I was born with will prevail when I lay them hands. I will look him in the eyes as I squeeze him into his last breath; he kept me from the woman I love, my only true wealth.

It seems I've been forgotten anyway. He passed me by, didn't even recognize my face. So, I will make myself my brother's keeper. With eyes burning with fire, I will become the grand reaper.

<u>Destiny's thoughts:</u>

I wonder if I have finally done too much, gone too far to turn back now. They say He can mend my broken heart, but I don't see how. My eyes begin to rain tears of sorrow down my face. I've looked everywhere and couldn't find grace.

This cold world has left me broken and bruised through rape, mo-lestation, abandonment, and shame. This anger I feel, you tell me where to put it and who to blame. I just want to feel a sense of peace, a normal life, but they say you only get to live once. Who made up this rule? You should get a do-over when needed and live it twice.

It's not fair; I have become the product of what was done to me. The lies, the monsters, and you say pray for my enemies. How can I pray for the one that I hate when I don't even pray for the one whose reflection I see?

I'm tired; I can't find a way out or for my soul to be at peace. The floodgates are open to my tears and inability. Unable to see past the pain and regret of this world. Lord, as I close my eyes, I just ask, when it's all over, don't forget about your girl.

Forgotten/Remember Me

Jay: (*two weeks later, in the hospital room*) How are you feeling, man? You seem to be zoned out today. You are really doing well, and it looks like you will be ready to come home.

DeVon: Nothing, man, I'm cool.

Jay: You better than cool, my guy. God has spared your life. A bullet to the heart that never pierced your heartbeat. A car that hit a pole and split in half, and yet, you are here with your whole body intact. The enemy came for you, my brother, and God spared you.

DeVon: Man, I don't want to hear all that spiritual stuff right now. I am here because it wasn't my time to go.

Jay: Right, you said it. So, you're talking spiritual stuff (*with a laugh*).

DeVon: I'm not talking about that man. It was a luck thing. God is not real.

Jay: My brother, the foolery of your speech can only be spoken through ignorance of the mind and pain in your heart. Your body is healing, but your heart and mind are dead. To not see the protection of God's hand on your life right now is a man with no wisdom. But I, my brother, believe, and I am so grateful for answered prayers that you will not speak against the power of my Father in my presence. I know what He did for you. I am a witness. I will not argue with you, but now begin to pray for your heart and mind the way I prayed for your body.

DeVon: Pray to who? The one that allowed me to be shot. The one that didn't protect me. You're talking about praying to change my heart; why didn't He change his if He had all the power?

Jay: Hey man, calm down. Don't get worked up. Your body can't handle the pressure.

DeVon: Don't tell me not to get worked up. I'm laid up in the hospital with a bag inside of me. My life was almost taken. (Shouting) Where the heck is Destiny?

Jay: I understand your pain. Don't worry; you will never see her again if I have anything to do with it. This is a clear sign that she is no good for you, man. You almost died in the name of so-called "love." You have got to let her go.

DeVon: (*sitting up in the bed, holding his stomach, and, with pain in his face, shouting*) Are you crazy? Why would you keep her from me? She had nothing to do with this.

Jay: Her husband shot you and caused you to crash your car. Is that not enough reason?

DeVon: No, he didn't. You have it all wrong. That man didn't shoot me.

Jay: What?

DeVon: I saw the guy that shot me. It wasn't him.

Jay: I don't understand. Your car hit a pole on the same street as her house. What were you even doing over there? We had just been praying for you that night, and I thought you were still in bed. You went to that man's house. (*With raised voice*) What were you thinking?

DeVon thought, *Jay has never raised his voice. He must be really upset. Let me talk calmly to him.*

DeVon: Look, Jay. I did go over there, only to let her know that we could no longer do this. That we had to try it the "right" way. You know the way you claimed *your* father wanted us to do. I really believed for those few hours. I remember lying on the bed and feeling so tired but peaceful. I had never felt that before. It was like my mind was talking to me for me. All it kept saying was, "Trust me and walk away while you can." (*crying now*). I fell asleep. When I woke up and saw that she had not even texted me, I panicked. It felt like something was wrong. I was still determined to do things the way *your father* said, but I loved her and needed to make sure she was ok. When she opened the door, I couldn't believe how much the love was still there. Just the sight of her calmed me. She was standing in that door with her eyes swollen from crying, and I needed to protect her. He wasn't home, so we just stood at the door and talked (*knowing he was lying, but there was no need to throw fuel on a fire*).

Jay: (*interrupting*) DeVon, are you telling me you stepped foot in that man's house? Your two feet went inside the door of this man's home to see about *his* wife. Are you serious? Do you understand the level of dishonor, disrespect, immorality, no wisdom, character, or integrity for yourself? You would stoop that low. You are more lost than I realized. So, intrigue me, my brother. Tell me how you ended up shot with a wrecked car on her street.

DeVon: I left and pulled up to the stop sign, and someone came up to the car, trying to rob me. I pulled off, and he shot at me. I don't remember anything after that.

DeVon's eyes shifted as he spoke that last sentence, and Jay's gut was telling him that something wasn't right. He couldn't take his boy's word for truth. He was confused because he had known DeVon to be many things but not a liar.

Jay: You know, man, I am going to let you get some rest. I need to run a few errands and go check on the house. Text me if you need me to bring anything back. I will see you this evening.

Sitting in a chair at the corner end of the hallway, Destiny saw

Jay get on the elevator. She didn't know how much time she had, so she ran to DeVon's room. To her surprise, he was sitting up in the bed looking out of the large picture frame hospital window at cars traveling the street in front of the hospital. He didn't realize she was there, and she was speechless to see him sitting up and in what appeared to be deep thought.

Destiny: DeVon, baby (*DeVon turned around and saw the only thing in life he cared about looking back at him. Destiny dropped her purse on the floor and ran to the hospital bed to hug him.*) Baby, I can't believe it. You're awake; you made it. I love you; I miss you so much, baby (*as she continuously kissed DeVon on his cheeks and forehead, she didn't realize that he hadn't said a word. She stood up and looked at him as he looked at her with confused eyes*). How are you feeling? What did the doctor say?

DeVon: (*angry*) Why do you care? Where have you been? Your husband tried to kill me because of my love for you, and you left me for dead!

Destiny: Baby, no, it's not that way at all. I have been here every single day and most nights. I knew Jay wouldn't let me stay because he thinks Chris did this to you, and apparently, so do you. I thought you told the police it was an attempted robbery. I'm so confused.

DeVon: (*remembering he did tell the police and Jay that story, and seeing Destiny cry struck a blow to his weakened heart. He reached for her hand*) Baby, I'm sorry, come here. Forgive me, I don't know what to think. I am just so confused about all of this. You don't understand what it is like to wake up in the hospital with a bullet in your chest with no idea how you got here.

Destiny: (*a little skeptical but sat on the side of the bed facing DeVon and held his hands, hands she wasn't sure she would ever touch again*). It's ok. I could only imagine. Please calm down, and don't get yourself worked up. Do you know how long Jay will be gone? I don't want him to come back and find me here. He was trying to get the police to press charges on me and Chris. I don't want to cause a problem in this hospital.

DeVon: It's ok; he won't be back until this evening. Please sit down so we can talk. I thought you had forgotten about me.

Destiny: Never in a million lifetimes. I have been praying night and day for your healing. I have given my life back to God. He has answered my prayers. A God that can hear my heart and my prayers has my life.

DeVon: *(bloodshot eyes and anger brewing in his heart)* Man, look, I don't want to hear about Him. I can't believe you believe in a magical being. (*Destiny looked extremely confused and caught off-guard*). You, Jay, and Angel can believe in the tooth fairies of the world if you want. But I am going to ask you to respect my wishes and don't bring it up around me. I believed in this so-called God that you guys talk so much about for a few hours. I truly felt something that I never felt before. But I guess that's a part of wishful thinking and hope that is in something non-existent. (*Sitting himself up in the direction of Destiny as she sat in a chair with eyes full of tears, he spoke firmly out of the very heart she begged God to heal*). Let me tell you something; if there really was a God, why is it that the minute I began to believe in Him and try to do the right thing, I almost lost my life? I was coming to your house to check on you, to share with you the hope I had. When I left, why did He allow me to be shot and crash my car? The only thing I had left in this raggedy world. Y'all say He healed me, but if He had the power to heal me, He also had the power to protect me, and He didn't. He only made my life worse! And you want me to love a person like that. You want me to believe He loves me? (*with an evil smirk, he continued*) Well, I tell you what; He apparently loves you, because regardless of you being a whoremonger, He kept you. You're still sitting up in your pretty house with a man paying all the bills. You have your car, your job, and everything else. Your life has not missed a beat. Meanwhile, I have lost my home, my job, my car, and most of all, my son over you! A piece of tail that ain't no different from the other skirts out here in these streets! You are good, but you ain't doing no real tricks to make a man be ok with dying for you. You know what? Maybe this needed to happen. It's time that I get control of my life again and show y'all how to do this.

Destiny: (*sobbing uncontrollably, thinking, Who is this monster, and where is DeVon?*) Baby.

DeVon: Don't call me that.

Destiny: DeVon, baby, your heart is...

DeVon: Did you hear what I just said? "Your baby" is what you never gave me and apparently what you could never give your husband. That's probably why he doesn't want you. You can't give a man a family because you're burnt up.

Destiny remembered that she would declare the name of the Lord in the earth and refused to go back on that promise, no matter what, even if the very reason she made the promise was for the man sitting before her tearing down everything he had built up inside of her during their love-encounter.

Destiny: You know, with all that you have said, I have a million thoughts, but I refuse to go there with you. You know how I know God is real? Because apparently, so is the devil, and he is all inside of you right now. I'm going to leave you two at it. You have forgotten. You have forgotten who you were and who I am. I will pray that your heart remembers. Remember who your grandmother said you were in the earth, God rest her soul. Remember who I was to you and the love that we shared with one another. You have a good afternoon, and yes, I will continue to pray for your healing!

Destiny, heartbroken and feet feeling like cement, grabbed her purse off the floor and walked out of the hospital room in shock. As she walked down the long hallway, her steps took her by the leading of the

Holy Spirit to the elevators. She was not present; only her body was, as she was consumed with her thoughts of what just happened and what she encountered from the man who looked like the man she loved but with eyes she didn't recognize. She thought to herself, *What was that?*

DeVon, left lying in bed with his thoughts, began conversing with himself. *Yeah, enough is enough. It's time for me to take charge again of my life. I did it before in my twenties out here in these streets. I had money, respect, and any woman I wanted besides Carolyn and Lil' Man* (he deep swallowed the pain he felt even at the thought of her and her son. With ego and pride risen to the occasion within his heart, he continued in thought). *Yeah, these streets have forgotten, but when I get out, I'm going to make them remember me!*

Be angry and do not sin; do not let the sun go down on your anger and give no opportunity to the devil (Ephesians 4:26-27, ESV).

Chapter Two

This Thing Called Life

Destiny's Thoughts:

Through a broken heart, I arise to the early morning sun that glows in darkness yet only through outward appearance. As I gather myself to get out of bed, tears begin to stream down my face. Before my lips ever speak a word, within minutes of the day, my heart feels heavier than my body.

The shower water brings no refreshing feeling to my face, only the ability to hide my tears. For a moment, I can just cry. As I use the towel to dry the water from my body, I wish I could also dry the pain. Yet, it's still present.

Swallowing every tear, fear, anger, and frustration of trying to understand why. What did I do to deserve this type of life? Why does it have to be so difficult? I sit on the foot of my bed with no energy to even get dressed for the day. I ask myself, "What am I doing? How did I get here?"

A Rain of Pain/Thunders of Regret

*S*itting on the ottoman at the foot of her bed, Destiny tried her best to dry her body and her tears. She reflected on yesterday's visit with something or someone looking like DeVon. She replayed the words in her head: "I have lost my home, my job, my car, and most of all, my son over you!" Her pain was interrupted by the doorbell. She thought to herself, *Who could this be? I just can't today.* Surprised at what her eyes were seeing, she tied her robe closed and opened the door.

Destiny: Chris, I wasn't expecting you today. What's going on?

Chris: I just came to pick up a few more things while in the area. Is that ok with you, Destiny? If not, I can come by another time.

Destiny: No, it's ok. Come in. Chris, you do know that I haven't changed the locks or anything. You can come and go as you please.

Chris: Oh, Noooo! We all know where that got us the last time I showed up unexpectedly to my own house. I'm good on that. I just want to grab some more things. I also want to discuss some of the clauses my attorney and I discussed regarding the divorce.

Destiny knew that was coming. Despite what DeVon thought, her world had also been turned upside down. While DeVon was in a coma for seven days, she and Chris had gone through a whirlwind of emotional highs and lows from being interrogated by the police continuously. They both lost their jobs because their pictures were posted on all news broadcasts and social media as "People of interest" in the case. And to add expected fuel to the fire of flames, Chris moved out and stopped paying the bills.

Destiny gestured for Chris to sit on the barstool at the kitchen island as she stood on the opposite side.

Destiny: Have a seat. Would you like something to drink?

Chris: Nope. I just need to grab a few things and advise you of a few things coming down the pipeline from my attorney.

Destiny: You're right. It is time to have this discussion. If I can first start off by saying I am sorry. I never meant for this to happen. I have asked myself a million times, "What was I doing? How the heck did I get here?" The truth of the matter is that we were living a life of lies and dishonesty. It finally caught up with us.

Chris: (*in disbelief*) We? I'm sorry; am I hearing you correctly? Are you trying to include me in your pity party of "I got caught up" blame? What did I do besides marry a woman who has no discretion? A woman who ran the streets and disrespected me and the home I provided for her by bringing her lover into the house that I paid for. Giving him the body that was in covenant with me. Only to leave, have a car wreck, get shot, and I be arrested and blamed for it. And you said, "We lived a life of lies." Do you have an alternate ego you meant that word "we" for?

Destiny: (*trying to stay humble*) Chris, I am not faulting you for DeVon's acci…

Chris: Don't say that man's name in my presence.

Destiny: I know you're not at fault for the accident or the shooting. You may be a lot of things, but you're not a killer. This I know. That is why I defended you to the police each time they questioned me. I have been doing a lot of reflecting and praying about our marriage: my indiscretions and yours. Whether you want to cop to it or not, we had anything but a marriage. I will admit that my actions were a reaction to your actions, and that is what has us here. We all played a role. I have asked God for His forgiveness. I have asked Him to give you favor so that you will not be charged for a crime that I know you didn't commit. I have asked Him to forgive us for what we have done.

Chris: You really have your nerves. You have changed all our lives, and you want to sit on your high horse of spirituality now. Where was all that praying when you were sleeping with him? Where was your spirit when you laid with this man in our home? I know I did some things to you, but never in our home. You were not the woman I thought you were. I regret the day I laid eyes on you. I cursed the day we said, "I do."

Destiny felt even more broken inside, the pain of accepting what she had done and caused too much to bear. With a soft voice, she tried hard to express herself to Chris.

Destiny: You know, Chris, this isn't easy. I'm so broken at this point; I can't do anything besides sit in it. The sad part is that you're not making it any easier. You refuse to sit in the failure of our marriage yourself. I…

Chris: (*with anger brewing in his heart and an entitlement of righteousness, he cuts Destiny off*). Girl, shut up! No one has an orchestra of sympathy playing for you. You got caught up in your adulterous ways, and like always, everyone is paying the price for your wrongdoings. You were born to scorn the lives around you. Hence, your child that is running around this world with no clue as to who her mother is. No wonder God doesn't allow you to be a mother; you don't know how to nurture anything but a hard pole in a man's pants.

Those words caused pain to rain through her veins like lava pouring out of an erupted volcano. How dare he speak on the broken place she shared with him during an intimate moment of their dating season. Within, Destiny shut down. Anger and rage arrived and pushed the pain aside. She became someone neither she nor Chris recognized.

Destiny: Let me tell you something, you piece of scrap of a sup-posed-to-be man! That's it! I have had enough of your…

Chris: (*getting up to walk to the back to grab some clothes*) Shut up; don't nobody want to hear it any…

Enraged and unable to take it anymore, Destiny reached her boiling point. She tried to do the right thing. She had prayed, she had taken accountability. She had let others express what they thought of her, remained humble, and apologized. She didn't start this Hell party by herself, but she may as well finish it! Sweet Destiny couldn't handle it, but Des could. Running behind Chris with a knife headed straight for his back, she let out a loud scream.

Destiny: I HATE YOUUUUUU!

Chris fell to the floor. He turned over on his back to see what was going on.

Des (speaking through Destiny): Let me tell you something, you little punk! She tried to be all you wanted and needed. She put up with your cheating ways; she put up with your disrespect of her as the woman of the house and her wishes concerning your father and his concubines. She dealt with the affairs of your friend's wife's daughter, your drunken behavior, and even calling her names. She keeps wanting to hold on to some hope and Jesus' stuff when I keep telling her to just take you out. Your life insurance policy is worth more than you. But she won't listen.

Chris was fearful because the eyes he was staring at assured him he was not dealing with weak Destiny. Someone else was in there. With an evil grin and laughter, she rubbed the knife against his cheek and continued to taunt Chris with threats of his life.

DeVon, he was good to us. And yes, it was easy to nurture the pole in his pants. I never understood what she saw in you. I knew she was just holding on to someone because she always wanted a sense of belonging. I was always there, but I wasn't good enough. From her mother and dad, family, and friends in school, I always tried telling her no one really cared about her but me. She just needed to keep feeding me, and I would protect her. So, I alienated her as a child; I convinced her no one cared. I whispered things in her ear to make her feel she was being talked about in school. We fought other kids like it was nobody's business. I thought I finally had her shell for myself when she had the one fight where she slammed the girl's head into the locker. I just knew that girl should have dropped dead, but she didn't, and Destiny only got suspended.

I finally convinced her she wasn't loved but that this boy would love her if she would just give him her body. I mean, I needed to be fed, and the connection of another body against mine was what I really needed. You must feed me for me to stay. (*Chris became more fearful but too scared to move, continuing to listen as Destiny straddled his chest with the knife to his throat*). She's a great listener, so she did. Her innocence was gone. I grew even larger. And once she had that bastard of a child and gave her away, I knew I was big enough to take control for a while. Finally, I had my own shell to walk around with and gain power in this earth. You see, all she really wanted was what she saw on that box y'all call a TV. I fool most of my victims that way. They spend their days and nights drooling over the hopes of having a life like what they see. How foolish y'all must be! You spend your time wishing for something that isn't real and forsaking what has been promised to you.

You're no different, Chris. You go from one woman to the next, feeding my flock with all that is within you. Spreading them every time you spread another woman's legs. You think you're the man. You can have as many women as you like, and you allow my kingdom to continuously be multiplied with what I need to fight the good fight in the end. Do you know how many women have become bitter and evil after the dealings of a man like you? The family structure has fallen to something as small as the size of your mind (*the evil laugh began again*).

And now, for the grand finale of one more soul lost for eternity at your hands, not hers. You broke someone that was already broken. You should have just let me handle it, but you had to be the man. For the price of one, I get to take two. Yours and hers. Welcome to my world!

***

For all that is in the world, the lust of the flesh, and the lust of the eyes, and the pride of life, is not of the Father, but is of the world. And the world passeth away, and the lust thereof: but he that doeth the will of God abideth for ever (1 John 2:16-17).

Chapter Three

<u>Stay in your Lane</u>

These roads are free, but both ways, the journey is long. It is almost guaranteed we will walk either path alone. The decision must be made a point of no return. The final destination, you get what you have earned.

Must I choose what I see vs. what could be, probability vs. possibility, facts vs. faith, what I have vs. what may be on the way? How does my mind take a road based on belief? When the road of my life has given me no relief. I can stay on a path and make my own way. This life has been hard enough, and someone has to pay.

I must choose one way or another, what I see vs. what I feel, what has happened vs. what has been revealed. The fact that my hurt, pain, and anger are real. I feel like I was cursed at birth with the seal.

One path tells me to keep going; vengeance is mine. The other path speaks in parables and calls himself the Divine. The choice to see vs. the choice to feel. The experience of the aftermath when the final judgment is revealed.

Intersection/Interception

*C*hris, trembling at what he was seeing and hearing, suddenly re-called a moment when he stood in his grandmother's kitchen, washing greens and listening to her talk to him about God. He had just run to her house after seeing his daddy beat his mom again. He couldn't understand why his mother would stay and deal with that. As he stood at the sink, his aging grandmother stood about 5 feet tall but always appeared to be tall to him. Her silver-gray hair was symbolic of the wisdom she spoke because she had experienced life and could help him to understand. But Grandma was getting old and weak. Hunched over the sink so her weight was held by its foundation, she said, her voice still solid and firm…

Grandmother: Baby, that old devil is a slickster. He will slide in you before you know it. He will also slide into the very one you love. He will use your heart's desire to break you. Yeah, make you do things you never thought you was capable of. That's why you must stay prayed up. Read the Word. So, when he comes, you will understand you're at war. The Bible says, "For we wrestle not against flesh and blood, but against principalities, against powers, against the rulers of the darkness of this world, against spiritual wickedness in high places."[1] So, you

---

must always be ready.

Remembering his grandmother's words while this thing continued straddling and taunting him, he, for the first time, took Grandma at her word. Grandma was a lot of things, but a liar she was not.

Chris: *(with authority in his voice)* The blood, the blood of Jesus, I rebuke you in the name of Jesus. Release me, get off of me. I am covered by the blood of Jesus.[2]

Immediately, Destiny looked at Chris with terror in his eyes and wondered why she was straddling him with a knife in her hand.

Destiny: (dropping the knife) What am I doing? How did I get here?

Chris, realizing it was her and not that thing, pushed her off him, jumped up, and headed toward the door. He told her in a gentle voice on his way out the door that she was demonic and needed to get help.

Destiny: Chris, what about your stuff?

Chris: *(running out the door and to his car, Destiny on his heels)* Don't worry about it. You can have it. In fact, you can have it all: the house, the furniture, my clothes, pictures. I don't want anything in that house.

Destiny: *(confused and tired of men running out the door for her to follow them)* Chris, we need to talk. I want a divorce as well, but I don't want to be enemies.

Chris: Girl, we are enemies. I don't want to be your husband, your friend; you know what, I don't even want to be your enemy. I just want to act like the last five years of my life never happened (*as he got situated in the car and started the ignition*). I will say this. Thank you. Thank you for showing up in a way that scared me into righteousness. I used to think my grandmother was Jesus crazy. She talked about Him all the time. I didn't see a need for Him because I couldn't understand

---

2   "Thou believest that there is one God; thou doest well: the devils also believe, and tremble." James 2:19, KJV.

if He existed and was as good as she said; why did He allow one half of me, my father, to be so evil towards the other half?

In that house, on that hallway floor, I just realized how. It has nothing to do with anything but what is inside of us. A person can be good and evil at the same time. All these years, I thought my dad never loved my mom. He just stayed with her because we were there, and he felt obligated. I would hear them argue with my mom that he loves her. I thought, surely, he was just trying to secure his spot in the house, but he sounded so convincing. And five minutes ago, I realized he was telling the truth. He did love her. But there was a monster inside of him that he could not control.

Destiny, for the record. You were a good woman; you were a great wife. I wouldn't have married you if I didn't think so. I do realize that the monster I had in me finally came to a head and pulled up the monster inside of you.

Destiny cried to the point that she was speechless. Chris had never taken any accountability for anything during their marriage. She had begun to think she was crazy and just didn't think normally regarding how a marriage should be, to the point she didn't believe she was worthy of a good husband because she wasn't a good woman. She was damaged goods from childhood. Chris, in a frail state of mind and realizing he had just had an encounter with the evil one, decided he would take the road less traveled, the one his grandmother always talked about. He was now vulnerable and honest, accepting of the part he played in getting Destiny to this point. He wanted in some way to right his wrong in case God was still listening after delivering him.

Chris: I knew you were broken when I met you. Here, this beautiful woman that I was initially scared to approach. Surely, she wouldn't deal with a man like me—gorgeous, confident, well dressed, good job. I watched as you walked into a store, and every man noticed you. The strange thing to me was that you were completely unaware of it. So, I shot my shot. The dating season was fun, but I realized that you were a woman with low self-esteem and seemed to be lonely. After a while, and I guess like-minded to my dad, I decided I would get you, wife you, house you, and if I could keep you in that broken place, I didn't have to worry about you going anywhere. You were under my control.

Now, looking back, I guess I was a bigger demon than the one that just confronted me. Destiny, several times in our marriage, you would have an attitude with me first thing in the morning for nothing. I was so baffled by how someone could wake up angry. That's why I would drink so early, to prepare for how you may wake up. I remember once you crying, saying things I had done the night before that I didn't remember. I attributed it to me being drunk and felt like you were exaggerating. Now I see that perhaps that same experience I just had was the one you were constantly experiencing, and I didn't remember anything.

He looked at Destiny's eyes, swollen with tears flowing continuously, but he knew in this uncomfortable state of feeling that he was doing the right thing.

You know, I remember, at the beginning of our marriage, how much you believed in God and was trying to live what you called an obedient life. I thought you were crazy just like my grandmother. Women used to kill me when they called themselves saved. They get so holy that it becomes a turn-off. I must admit, there is something to it. I can't deny it.

He shut off the car and stepped out to face Destiny. He was no longer afraid because he was familiar with the eyes that were looking back at him.

Let me do something I never did in our marriage. Destiny, sweetheart, you had it right back then. The way you felt, the times you prayed, the concerns you had regarding me. You were on the right path. You were not crazy. I was doing the things you felt I was doing. I enjoyed the life of having the women I wanted for fun and someone to keep the house up for me while I was doing my thing. It was my goal to keep you broken and in pain.

Another thing, when I found out about DeVon, I was livid. I had known of you having a friend here and there and decided I would let you have a little fun since I was doing my thing. But the intent was to have fun and come back home. With this dude, I felt you slipping away. You no longer cared about what I was doing. You stopped arguing and agreed with whatever I said. There were many nights I came home on lunch in the middle of the night to find you gone. The next morning, instead of being an angry woman, you were happy, cooking breakfast and walking around the house singing. You were back to being the woman I first married. But I knew I wasn't responsible for the smile on your face any longer.

That night of the accident, DeVon did see my face. When I left, I pulled down the street to watch the house because I knew someone was there. Before I could turn the car off, I saw him running out the door and you following him, begging for something. Imagine seeing your wife run after another man, begging him to stay. I was furious. I saw him pull out of the driveway, and I instantly followed him. I honestly don't know what happened. It seems like he just lost control of the truck, and he hit a tree. In my anger, I got out and ran up to his truck, ready to beat his.… Well, I wasn't sure what I was going to do, but I did want to put my hands on him. When I saw him, he had taken enough beating from that tree. I looked at him, and he looked at me, and, at that moment, I decided he got what he needed, and I turned and walked away. No, I wasn't going to help him; I didn't care if he lived or not. But I did not put my hands on him, let alone shoot him. The police tested my gun, and there was no gunpowder residue because I never pulled it out, let alone pull the trigger.

Destiny: *(shocked at all that she is hearing and, having trouble with where to start, allows her heart to speak)* Chris, I am not sure what to say. There's so much I want to say, but I'm not sure what. But Chris, why would you allow him to lay there injured and not help?

Chris: I am not sure, but I do know as much as I didn't want to help him, I didn't want to cause more harm, either. You know, the more I talk, it seems like when something major happens, it's like these pivotal moments of life where you come to this crossroads, a point in which you can go one of two ways. You can take one road or the other. No matter what, you must decide you can't just keep going the way you're going. That is not an option! There were times that I took the wrong road and went from bad to worse. Like how I was treating you. And then there are those moments like when I saw him and wanted to put my hands around his neck and take his very last breath myself. I wanted to be God and make the final decision on his life, but I couldn't. Every fiber of my being made me turn and walk away. Oddly enough, those moments always made me feel at peace. So, when the police came, I didn't worry. I knew in my heart I did nothing wrong. *(opening the door to get back in his car and start the engine).* Even though this road sometimes makes me feel like my pride is being stripped of me, it always comes with a sense of calmness that I can't deny. After seeing what I just saw in that house, I can't lie to myself any longer. This world can have my pride; I don't mind being stripped of this ego. Heck, it can even have these lustful eyes.

I chose the one that just kept me and protected me even though I was not deserving. I chose the one that allowed me to see the reality of my death yet allowed me to live. I chose the one that will forgive me for all that I have done and has had mercy on my soul, even during my foolishness all these years. I knew you were broken when I met you. Instead of affirming you, I dug further into the hole that now sits in your heart. Please forgive me for what I have done. So that you can move on, please forgive me, and I pray that God will forgive me too.

With nothing left to say and feeling drained, Chris pulled out of the driveway in hopes of never returning to this point of life and to this house again. He was willing to give it all up to take the road less traveled.

***

"If my people, which are called by my name, shall humble themselves, and pray, and seek my face, and turn from their wicked ways; then will I hear from heaven, and will forgive their sin, and will heal their land" (2 Chronicles 7:14, KJV)

Chapter Four

<u>Rivalry Spirits</u>

DeVon Thoughts:

You plotted, you schemed, kept my mind in wheels. The deception of my life was your thrill. You lied to me, whispering pain in my ears. I was tormented for days, weeks, and years.

Believing what you said, what you whispered in my heart. The fire grew big, the cold cemented walls built around my heart. You do come to kill, steal, and destroy—your lies I refuse to believe anymore.

Jay Thoughts:

I can't believe it's you. I can't believe you're real. You were there all along; those nights my heart couldn't feel. I cried out; I asked so many times why. Although the pain was real, your divinity I couldn't deny. My father, I submit to you humbly. I believe that you come that I may have life abundantly.

The Devil's Plot/ God's Plan

DeVon had been discharged from the hospital and was at Jay's and Angel's home again. As he sat at their kitchen table, picking over the food that Angel had cooked for him, he didn't have an appetite. He reflected on the conversation he had with Destiny. And although he missed her dearly, the first task at hand was revenge.

DeVon's thoughts: *I'm over it; I am over it all. Heck, I may as well add Destiny to the I'm-over-it list. I tried to be the good boy like Jay, so I can get me a wife, too. But that ain't my story. No matter how hard I try, my life always ends in hurt or pain caused by someone other than myself. What Jay must realize is that everyone is not born with the good life assigned to them. I was born under a curse. My daddy stepped out on his wife and loved my momma. Love took both of their lives. So, what is love other than trouble and pain? That man doesn't see it for himself. There is no telling what Angel is out here doing behind his back. Truthfully, I doubt it. They were born with the gift of a good life, and I...well, this is my story. I belong to the one that I tried to run from, and now I am running to him. He is the only one that gets me. (DeVon is suddenly interrupted from his thoughts).*

Jay: Hey man, you ok?

DeVon: Yeah, man, what's going on?

Jay: Nothing much. I kept calling your name. You in deep thought?

DeVon: Something like that.

Jay: You care to share.

DeVon: Not really. Just trying to figure some things out in my head. Got a lot to try and do. I need to get a job, a car, and a place to stay. I appreciate how good you and Angel have been, but I'm a grown man, and this ain't my life.

Jay: No, it's not your life. It's just the season you are in right now. This too shall pass.

He pat DeVon on his shoulder as he walked past his chair and sat down at the table across from him. DeVon, turning his head to look out the window, spoke in a whisper.

DeVon: Here we go again.

Jay: What was that supposed to mean?

DeVon: I'm just saying, man, I don't want to hear it. Don't make all those spiritual comments to me. Those days—rather, few hours—of believing are behind me now.

Jay: Playboy, I can understand your hurt and pain. But what I am confused about is why you are mad at God. What did He do wrong besides heal your body and not your wacky mind? *(Trying to crack a joke that fell on deaf ears).*

You said yourself this was a robbery gone bad. Truthfully, you should have never been on that street. We are not even going to discuss that house. So, it's only fair to say that even in your wrongdoing, we must give God the glory for keeping you when the enemy came for you. It's just time to heal and move on.

DeVon: *(with piercing eyes, he looked into Jay's soul)* You think it's that simple? You are more simple-minded than I thought. That wasn't protection. Protecting someone is keeping them from hurt, harm, and danger. You think it was protection? Man, let me tell you something. It was him. *(Jay looked confused.)* Yeah, it was Mr. Hubby, Chris. I left that house, telling the woman I love that I was done with her for good. Trying to do as you say, "the right thing," and a car came up behind me so fast that all I could see was a light. I hit a tree before I knew it. That man had the nerve to walk up to my truck while I was lying upside down and at the end of my life, and he looked at me eye to eye. The last thing I saw was his face until I woke up seven days later from a coma to find that he not only made me hit a tree, but he wanted to make sure he finished me off and shot me.

Where is the protection in that? Where is this God you talk about in that? That man plotted to take my life, and God was just going to let him.

Jay: (still confused) Well, why did you tell the police someone robbed you?

DeVon: I don't need him in jail. I need him walking these streets. I don't need a court system. (*with evilness in his eyes*) I'm the prosecutor, the jury, and the judge. I will handle his sentence.

Jay recognized what he saw in DeVon's eyes. He was not fearful at all. In fact, he had waited his entire spiritual walk for a moment like this.

Jay: Man, let me explain something to you. You are falling right into the plot of the enemy. This is exactly what he wants you…

Still in pain, DeVon slowly got up to try to walk out of the kitchen. DeVon was on his heels right behind him as they entered the living room, where Angel was sitting on the couch watching TV.

DeVon: Man, shut up. Don't nobody want to hear…

Jay: Hold on, playboy. Gather yourself. This is still my house, and you will respect me in my house. I have been here and haven't left your side once. Whether you agree with me or not, you will respect my house.

Angel: *(confused and concerned for DeVon's well-being, she stands up from the couch)* What is going on? Why are y'all yelling? DeVon, please sit down. You are in no condition to be stressing yourself.

DeVon, knowing he would never disrespect his brother's wife and realizing the pain was getting stronger, sat down on the black recliner. It was the same recliner that he sat in for hours after they fell out about Destiny just three weeks ago. The same chair he sat in for a few hours before the attempt on his life. He may have been mad, but he did feel like that night; he should have listened to them and stayed in bed. He would have never been further in the hole than he was now. Angel helped the two men find where to sit, and she sat on the other end of the couch between Jay and DeVon. She turned the television off.

Angel: Now, what is the problem? Why are you guys fussing?

Jay: This man had the audacity to disrespect me in my own…

DeVon: Man, ain't nobody disrespecting you. My disagreement is not disrespect. You just don't like what I am saying. I have a right to how I'm feeling.

Jay: (*with his voice raised to meet DeVon's*) You have a right to this as…

Angel: Hold on, hold on, hold on! Y'all stop it right now. I am telling you this…

Jay: (*with an authoritative voice*) Baby, sit back. We are grown men. I will handle this.

Angel: (*giving him a look that made him sit back on the couch and be quiet. Speaks in a respectful but motherly tone*) Jayyyyyyy, I need you to get yourself together, and I mean quickly. Watch your tone with me, sir. I'm in this one because this is my house, too. Secondly, DeVon, you are like a brother to me, and I refuse to sit back and let the two of your egos go to war with each other. Thirdly and most importantly, I am trying to watch *Divorce Court,* and y'all are messing up the only ratchet 30 minutes of fun I have in a day! So, if y'all don't sit your simple-minded selves down and figure this out, I am going to have a problem. And neither one of you can beat me in having a problem. You can bet your last dollar on that! (*Calmly, she continued.*) Now, what seems to be the problem?

Jay: Do you know this man admitted that he knows that girl's husband shot him? He lied to the police. After all he had done with this man's wife and in his home, he has the nerve to be talking about taking revenge into his hands.

DeVon sat, not saying a word, just looking at the wall. He was more embarrassed now than he was angry. He never wanted anyone to know he knew. Especially Jay and Angel, who he knew would try and talk him out of it. He loved them and respected them. He had nobody left in this world but them, and he didn't want to lose them also. They just needed to respect his beliefs, and he would allow theirs. Angel was looking at DeVon.

Angel: DeVon, is that true? Please tell me it's not true. Look at me, DeVon (*with a stern voice*). Look me in my eyes and tell me it's not true.

DeVon: (*not able to lie to Angel or even raise his voice at her*) Look, Angel, I am not trying to disrespect you (*making a point to look at Jay also*) or you guys' home. The truth is, I love the both of you. I have been so lucky to have friends…I mean, a sister and brother like the two of you in my life. You guys don't understand this type of pain. Since I was born, there is like this curse that is over my life. I don't know if it's because of the institution I was born in or what. But everyone is not born with God's grace and mercy that you both talk about. You guys have it so easy—such a beautiful life. You're married; you come home to one another. You laugh and hang out together. The hardest part of your lives is fighting about who's going to cook dinner.

My parents were killed when I was ten—just taken away like it was nothing for me to be left behind. The only person I had left was my grandmother. I listened to her talk about this same God that you all talk about, but we barely had food to eat. I watched her lie as if she wasn't hungry so that I could eat whatever she was able to muster up. Yet, you want me to believe in this God.

On her deathbed, I learned that I had no other family because I wasn't accepted by my father's family at no fault of my own. Why did I have to pay the price for their mistakes? Their lives taken should have been enough.

DeVon's eyes filled up with tears at the very thought of the one who got away 20 years ago when he was younger. He still had to swallow his pain before her name could come out of his mouth.

And then, to add insult to injury, Carolyn and Samuel, who was like the family that I was given as a settlement of pay for all the pain I endured, were snatched from me.

I spent three years of my life in prison. I get out. Try to become an honest man. I get a job, a car, and a place to stay. But there is still something missing. It's gnawing at me day and night. I was lonely and just wanted to feel love. Feel a woman's touch in more ways than a "friend with benefit" kind of way. See her smile when I walk through the door. Taste a homecooked meal. Have someone to be lazy with on the couch and watch TV. Fall asleep in each other's arms only to wake up the next day and do it all over again. That was all I wanted.

With tears still falling but DeVon's words clear, Jay and Angel continued to listen, holding on to every word he spoke. They knew DeVon needed to get this out.

And then, finally, I meet a woman who makes me feel like a man. A woman who lights up when I walk in the room. I feel in my heart I'm wanted and needed. When I look into her eyes, I lose all ego and pride. But she comes with baggage. Baggage that I feel I can handle because I know my love will make her leave him and come to me, where she's wanted. That man didn't deserve her love. How can you have a treasure like that and treat it like the bottom of your shoe? She needed me as much as I needed her.

You know, when I was lying in my truck, my body crushed between the seat, steering wheel, and window, he looked me in the eyes. You know what I saw? I didn't see a man that was hurt by his wife's infidelity. I saw pride and ego. You want to know how I know what it was. I could imagine it was the very thing that man saw in me when I shot him at Carolyn's apartment. The energy in the air was too familiar to deny. In him was entitlement and righteousness for what was happening. I saw someone that was getting off on my pain and suffering. Whatever that was in him wanted me to die. It was getting pleasure in seeing me become lifeless. And the God that you guys had just talked to me about was not there. He did not protect me. He did not cover me. He did not stop it from happening. You said He knows the heart. He knew when I went there, in my heart, I only wanted to check on her. My heart was worried about her. My heart wanted to let her know that we had to do this the right way. Yet, He let it all unfold.

(He straightened himself up and dried the last of his tears).

So, forgive me if I am having trouble agreeing with you guys after my life has been tested and proven that He is not real. Well, let me correct myself. He is real; I'm just not one of His. So, if I don't belong to Him and there are only two powers at work, then who do you think I belong to?

Angel: *(with understanding eyes and a humble voice)* DeVon, none of us belong to the enemy. None of us! But given the life you've had, I can understand your questioning of it all. This life is so hard, and most of the things that happen to us we didn't ask for, such as our parents.

I also must be honest and say some of the pains of our lives are also a direct result of the decisions we have made. Decisions can be so dangerous when they are made without thought of consequences and repercussions, when they are not made based on our foundational principles. We have all been there. We have all made some foolish decisions that can destroy us because we have no idea of the plot that is against all of us from birth.

I know you look at us and think we have it all together. But the fruit that you now see is the outcome of the foundation on which we decided we would build our lives individually and as a couple. That foundation is the word of God. It looks beautiful because He has the power to make all things new, including us as people. He doesn't allow us to look like what we have gone through. But don't be deceived. We have both individually gone through some things you couldn't imagine.

I know you know firsthand what you saw in that man's eyes. The energy you speak of that you felt. But to everything, there is an opposite. To darkness, there is light; to pain, there is peace; and to evil, there is goodness. *(She stood up to leave the two men to talk as she turned to Jay).* I think, baby, it's time for you to share with DeVon what you looked like before you found that peace he sees in you. Share with him the reason for your hope.

Angel went upstairs knowing that if God be lifted up, He would draw DeVon unto Him. She was just hoping she could replay *Divorce Court* and get a chance to laugh. *All this foolery going on in this house.* She thought to herself, *no wonder God hasn't given us any kids. Jay and DeVon are like children. And it is all I can handle in this house. I may as well cook hot dogs or chicken nuggets for dinner.*

Jay and DeVon sat quietly for a few seconds after Angel left the room. They were left with their thoughts. DeVon felt drained and thought that this had gone in a direction he didn't want.

Jay thought, *could this be the moment that God allows his testimony to serve a purpose in the Kingdom?* He loved his brother DeVon, but he loved God more and refused to be quiet for the sake of fake peace. He quietly said a prayer to himself. *"Father, let the words of my mouth, the meditation of my heart be acceptable in thy sight. Speak through me, use me as you feel, and speak to DeVon's heart. In Jesus' name, I pray. Amen."*

Jay: Hey, man, do you need anything? You need some water or your pain meds?

DeVon: Nah, I'm good. Besides, I am too scared to get out of this chair. I feel like my mother told me to sit down and shut up (*snickering*). Angel might catch you, but she won't catch me.

Both men laughed, and it broke the energy in the room, welcoming in peace.

Jay: Yeah, that woman is something else. God knew what He was doing the day I went to that park on Langston Avenue. Who would have thought? You know she spoke the truth. I know sometimes I come on strong about my beliefs. It's only because my mind is still blown at who and what I was and who and what I am now. I wasn't always like this.

DeVon: *(in shock with a relaxed, laughing tone)* It seems like you were breaded and buttered in this faith thing.

Jay: I'm shocked myself sometimes, but I have a reason. You know our stories may differ, but that pain is the same. You met me once I had gotten it together, during the beginning fruits of the decision I made to follow Christ. Had you seen me even a year before that, you probably wouldn't have believed my transformation.

DeVon sat back in the recliner. He realized that after all these years of knowing Jay, he had never known who he was before they met and what his life was like. He found himself interested in what Jay had to say. Besides that, anger and bitterness were draining. He was too tired to do anything but listen. His mind was made up, but he loved his boy, and for that reason, he cared about his story.

Jay: You know, when I first met Angel, I had ulterior motives, but after a while, I thought to myself, "It's about time something good is happening in my life." We began to date, and she just felt right. Trust me, man, I didn't want her to be. I fought hard with myself. But she was what I liked and what I wanted. A year into the relationship, we moved in together.

DeVon: *(being sarcastic)* I know the saved folks wasn't living in sin.

Jay: *(laughing and getting comfortable on the couch)* Shut up, man. I told you we were not always saved. Anyway, I was thinking that things were going well, and I knew she was the woman I wanted to marry. She had her issues. Lord knows, her mouth was foul at times. But at her core, she was beautiful inside out. So, we would have arguments here and there, and although it wasn't constant, it felt like World War III when it happened.

One of our most repeated arguments was her telling me that I was mean. I seemed angry all the time. I couldn't understand why she was saying that because I was ten times nicer to her in comparison to others *(both men laughing).* I didn't like people; I didn't trust them, and the last thing I wanted to do was be around them. But after a while, it bothered me that the woman I love saw me as an angry man. I hadn't even considered how my anger was showing up in our relationship. One argument had my blood pressure so high that I felt like my head was going to explode.

You know, I always had empathy for you regarding your parents and their life ending so abruptly. I could understand your hurt. But I used to think to myself, at least you had ten good years of love with them. But what do you do when the very one that had you is the one that you need protection from? That you are only good for being a servant.

So, after that argument, I laid back in that very chair you are sitting in and thought to myself, "What am I doing? How did I get here?" Whew!!! My mind took me back to when I was a child. I couldn't have been no older than nine or ten when my mom had my sister.

DeVon was shocked. For the first time, he heard his boy's voice going weak. It was not a space he was familiar with or comfortable with. He was used to holding the title of weakness in their friendship. However, he watched as Jay appeared to go into another place as he reflected on his past.

Jay, at Nine Years Old

Jay was in bed asleep when he was suddenly awakened by a hit upside his head.

Jay's Mom: Boy, get up and feed this baby. Get up now and go fix her bottle.

Jay: Momma, I got to go to school in the morning.

Jay's Mom: The only thing you got to do is get this baby a bottle and get her back to sleep; now, here! (*Hands Jay the baby*). And don't say another word.

Jay stumbled out of bed and to the kitchen. By then, he had become a pro at putting the bottle in a pot with water until it boiled, then pulling the bottle out and testing to see if it was too hot on the back of his hand before sticking it in Pumpkin's mouth. He certainly didn't want to feel his mother's wrath for not getting the temperature of the bottle right. Once he had settled into the chair next to an end table that held a red lamp with a bright light, he began to feed his baby sister, rocking back and forth as if he had done this his entire life. He preferred sitting in this chair because he noticed that Pumpkin (as he lovingly called her) liked staring at the light from the lamp as she drank her bottle.

As he rocked her, he thought to himself how tired he would be at school tomorrow. It was 1:00 in the morning, and chances were that Pumpkin wouldn't be going back to sleep for at least an hour. So that meant *he* wasn't going to sleep for at least an hour. Starring at Pumpkin as she drank the bottle, Jay was so confused with his feelings. How could he love someone so much and dislike them at the same time? He loved his baby sister. But her being here was now another added stress of him having to deal with his mother, even though his mother was the one that laid in entertainment of creating Pumpkin, carried her for nine months, and birthed her in the world. One thing was for certain: Pumpkin was Jay's responsibility. As he patted her back, he prayed that she would burp so she could go back to sleep. He just wanted to be able to think clearly for school the next day. He dealt with the cruelty of life at home, but his "don't play; I will whoop you like I created you" uncle was his biggest concern. Jay's mom didn't care about his schooling, but he had an uncle who would put his foot in his tail if he didn't make the right grades. While rocking Pumpkin, one thing Jay knew for sure, in this lifetime, besides his sweet grandma Dea', was that he couldn't win for losing.

Dea' was about five feet tall with thick, straight, silver hair. Her Indian facial features were proof that her hair was all hers. She passed those good genes down even to Jay. You could look at Dea' and tell that although she had lived a long life, she lived a good one. Most of all, she lived a wise one. Jay thought to himself that maybe Dea' stuck around to take care of Mother because she knew that something was off. If nothing else, she was Jay's protector. Mother hated the fact that Dea' loved Jay so much.

Dea': Baby, get on up now. Come on, you got to get up before you miss the school bus.

Jay: Yes, ma'am.

Later that evening, Jay returned home from school at peace and happy because the last eight hours of his life were normal. And the school cookies and milk always made everything ok. Most kids didn't care for the lunches at school, but it was the joy of his day because he loved eating. Those were happy times. As Jay walked in the door, even as a child, he could feel the energy in the house was off. His mother had a temper and was known for fighting anyone, from a boyfriend to the neighbor across the street. Everyone knew Jay's mom could throw those hands. Jay walked into the kitchen, where his mother stood with an angry posture and ready to skin someone alive, and Jay was not exempt because he was her son. As he stood trying to answer all her questions sensibly, he saw his mother grab the wooden fork that hung on the wall as décor and head in his direction. His confusion caused him to freeze, and with one swipe, blood was drawn.

Mother: Get out, get out of here, now!

Jay: But what did I do? (*His mom shoving him towards the front door*) Where am I supposed to go?

Mother: I don't care where you go; get out of my house now!

Jay sat in confusion as his mother pushed him onto the front porch and slammed the door. He did not understand what was going on, just as any other time she had lashed out at him. Perhaps she hated that he was born. Perhaps she was upset because things didn't work out with his dad. Even that thought was confusing for Jay because she chose her dad, not him.

Jay sat on the porch until evening turned to night. Roughly about midnight, his grandmother did what she always did: come and get him, bring him back in, feed him something, rub his head, and send him on to bed. Dea' had the ability to make all things right, just from being in her presence. Jay had no idea what happened and how Dea' could have a child like his mother, but he oftentimes felt just as sorry for her as she did him. They were in this together.

Jay, as a teenager a few years later

Jay's mom had a few more kids for him to take care of. It had gotten to a point where he learned to time himself in the morning for school. His mom's new trick in the bag was to make him go to the store before school to get her cigarettes, and if he missed the school bus, *oh well*. He needed to stay home and watch the other children anyway. Oddly, Jay did great in school, mainly because he enjoyed learning. He absorbed the studies of history as if he actually lived in those days. It didn't hurt that his other incentive was having to answer to an uncle who loved him enough to require him to get good grades in school and act like he had a normal life, even when he didn't.

But time was passing, and now it was time for Pumpkin to start kindergarten as well. Jay was used to being teased about not having new school clothes or even holes in his shoes. It was ok because he was just as good at telling jokes as the kids that had on the new sets. Plus, just like his mom, he was known for being able to lay those hands, too. He only had to stand his ground for a little while. Classmates soon learned he wasn't an easy "bully" walk in the park. However, he was now in middle school and couldn't be at Pumpkin's school to protect her. She was going to be by herself until he got to her in the evening. There were a lot of decisions that kids like Jay had to make when they were in the hood and faced with adversity that was bigger than they could handle.

Looking around the neighborhood and seeing the gangsters and dope boys with all the money, the cars, and the clothes seemed to be a good lifestyle for a 15-year-old young man who needed food and clothes. He had a great excuse now. He had a child he must take care of. Pumpkin will not go through what he went through.

Chapter Five

<u>When Sunday Morning Comes</u>

I stand at the back door, frozen, arrested by the motionless spirit of my feet. I see an usher. She points to me. By the signal of her hand, she lets me know she has a seat for me.

I see her, but I scan the room. Still unable to move, I grip tight my bag. Everything appears to be in slow motion. As the choir sings, they sound muffled and distant, as if they are worshipping the Father underwater.

I walk down the center with my floodgate of tears, past the pews, past the ushers, past the motherboard to the altar. I fall to my knees. Drenched in my tears, I open my bag and pour out all the pieces of my shattered heart. I can't speak a word; I can't call out. I can't think of a prayer. The very breath I took was pushed out by grace. I knew at that moment I couldn't even breathe.

Finally, I opened my mouth and said, "Father, I am sorry. The heart you gave me is broken and shattered. Please forgive me and make me whole again. Please take this pain away. The enemy has come to take my life away. I can't go on another moment; I can't go another day. Lord, there has to be another way."

With swollen eyes and tear ducts that won't dry, I will beg God for a new heart when Sunday morning comes.

The Mind vs The Heart

Destiny was drained. It had been a week since her incident with Chris and even longer since she had talked with DeVon. She had cried, screamed, replayed her life in her head, prayed, burned sage, and brought crystals. Nothing eased the pain she was feeling in the depths of her heart. Some nights, she was scared to go to sleep because her heart was so fragile, she was afraid she wouldn't wake up.

She called that one friend who would remind her that "you only live once," who would get her focused again on the good times and having fun.

Destiny: *(the phone rings)* Hello, Zondra. Is that you?

Zondra: Hey girl, look what the wind blew in. How are you doing?

Destiny: I have no idea how I am doing. How are you?

Zondra: I'm good. Living my best life. Out here catching flights, not feelings.

Destiny: Teach me, girl, teach me how.

Zondra: Where are you right now? Come up here to Scales. I'm at the bar having a drink.

Destiny: Drop your location. I am on my way.

Destiny jumped up from the couch and ran to the room to get dressed. Finally, some normalcy was about to come back into her life.

Maybe those crystals were working. For a moment, she began to think that she had just spent money on mere decorations.

She tried to remember all the rules of the bar set. Get cute but casual. She wasn't looking for a man; in fact, it was the last thing she wanted right now, but rules are still rules. Plus, she may be getting ready to jump back into the single pond party and needed to make sure she was a catchable fish. At the very thought of not having DeVon, she had to swallow her pain again. Her heart began to burn again, and she immediately sat on the side of the bed to massage away the pain in her heart. Sometimes, you just have to massage your heart to keep it pumping through this type of hurt.

Finally, she arrived at her "do-over" future. She took one last look in the review mirror and got out of the car.

The two women embraced as if they hadn't seen each other in ages. Well, they hadn't. Destiny realized she hadn't seen Zondra since the week before DeVon's accident.

Destiny: *(as she settles at the bar)* Zondra, girl, I have missed you. You look gorgeous. How do you get prettier with time?

Zondra: *(laughing and soaking in all the compliments.)* Girl, it's the newest edition to my rooster. This one is a personal trainer, and he is personally training me.

(The women burst out in laughter).

Destiny: Can I get one that will allow me to eat carbs?

Zondra: So, what has been going on with you? The only glimpse of you I get is a picture of you and your husband scattered across the news. I finally gave up calling since I wasn't getting a callback. You ready to talk now?

Destiny: *(the mood suddenly changes, and the cloud is now at the bar.)* Girl, what hasn't gone on? It's been so much, Zondra. My heart is so broken, and I don't know what to do. Long story short, DeVon came by the house about a month ago. While he was there, Chris came home unexpectedly. I had to hide DeVon in the closet. When Chris left, DeVon left immediately, screaming it was over. He got in his truck and pulled off. I went into the house; I was so upset and crying. I was on the couch when I heard sirens like crazy. I looked out the window and saw the police and an ambulance all over the beginning of our street. I laid back down, and my heart couldn't stop wondering what it was because DeVon had just left, and they were not out there then. I called him a few times, but he didn't answer as I expected he wouldn't have. Finally, I got up and put some clothes on to run to the store to get some wine, and as I was coming up to the cross street to turn and avoid the crowd, I realized it was DeVon's car turned upside down.

(Zondra grabbed her chest in shock as she held on to every word).

Zondra: What happened? Is he ok?

Destiny: He is alive, but he is not ok. He not only hit a tree, but he was shot also *(Zondra gives a side-eye look)*. I see that look; it wasn't Chris. I talked to Chris, and he said he had seen the wreck but that he had nothing to do with it. DeVon just lost control of the car, and I am not sure what happened with him being shot. The news says it was a robbery gone wrong. Either way it goes, he hates me, and Chris hates me now. So, once again, I am right back where I started from.

Zondra: What are the odds of him getting robbed on your street? You don't really believe that, do you?

Destiny: Chris said he didn't do it, and I believe him.

Zondra: You also believe that love is real. You also believe in fairytales, unicorns, and rainbows. You also believe all that mess you see on TV. You believe everything that you shouldn't. And now you think this man didn't have anything to do with that boy being shot! You are crazy.

Destiny was confused and embarrassed because people were starting to look. Zondra's voice was a level above the music and caused a scene. In fact, this was the first time she had ever seen Zondra angry, and she was trying to figure out who she was mad at.

Destiny: Zondra, can you lower your voice? People are looking.

Zondra: *(Realizing she was causing a scene, she gathered her emotions together.)* Girl, you just got me all out of character. Look, when we first met, I thought it was cute how you looked at the world and saw the innocence of everyone around you. I believe you could make the devil not seem so bad. But, sometimes, sis *(using her hand to lift Destiny's chin as she sat at the bar facing her in shame),* your best attribute can be your worst. This "the world is beautiful and everyone in it" outlook you have is now bringing harm to others with no accountability. Don't let Chris' plea of innocence make you forget the monster he was to you. A woman that didn't do him any harm, and yet he treated you like the bottom of his shoe. Do you think for one minute that he wouldn't attempt to take the life of a man who was with his wife and in his house? Don't be that blind, Des. Open your eyes and see what is going on.

Destiny, now at the bar in full cry mode, wiped her tears enough to flag the bartender to close out her tab. Deep down, she knew Zondra was right. No matter how much she tried to convince herself that Chris wouldn't do anything like that, it just didn't add up.

Zondra: Des, look, I am sorry that I have to be the dream killer. Through your eyes, I almost had hope for a minute last year. You started making me think maybe I should give this love thing a try. You and DeVon did make a good couple. He did love you in a way that gave me hope just watching. Then I went home, and reality was waiting for me. I knew that was your life, not mine. I knew better, and so for me, life just kept on life-ing.

For the first time, Destiny just couldn't receive that message from Zondra. Destiny may not know what was wrong, but she knew what was right, and she refused to let her heart go there again. Believing in Zondra's makeshift life was draining. Maybe everyone does take different roads to get to the final destination. Destiny snickered as she thought to herself, *We have to go through all of this in life and still have to die. Wow!*

Destiny: *(as she gathers her things to leave Zondra at the bar)* Zondra, I truly love you. Perhaps you are right, and I am the crazy one. But I can't deny that somewhere deep inside my body, like the blood that flows through my veins, I just believe in love. I believe it as if I can breathe it. I can't explain it, and that is why I can accept that it sounds crazy. But at this point, I would rather be crazy and open myself up for what is eating at me than ignore what I believe to be the very essence of my being.

I'm tired, sis. I have tried everything I can think of. I have tried imitating the life I see on TV. I have tried hanging out in these raggedy streets, going from bar to bar and club to club. I have tried having a husband and a boyfriend. I have purchased clothes and makeup, and none of these things are getting me to where I thought I would be. In fact, it seems like I'm going in the opposite direction, and this road is draining.

There is nothing left for me to try other than the one that created me. Maybe it's not Him that's being quiet, and yet it's my heart so clogged up with other things that I cannot hear Him. I don't know, but I do know that, as a child, He gave me peace. When I was married to Chris and really trying to be a good wife, I was at peace, regardless of what Chris was doing. That was the only place where my mind was quiet, and my heart was at peace. Yeah, I think I would rather have that again; his track record is undefeated in my life.

Zondra smiled at her friend as she held her drink, because she would be sitting right at this bar scouting for players to add to her roster when Destiny leaves. She looked with pitiful eyes at Destiny because she knew in her heart Destiny was just built that way. And she had to let her friend make her mistakes. She couldn't teach her or protect her from anything else.

Zondra: Awe, here go, baby girl, with the rainbow and unicorn dreams again. That is ok, sweetie. Somebody got to believe for the both of us. If it doesn't work out, call me. I have a few on my roster I could loan you.

Destiny and Zondra hugged. As she walked out the doors of Scales, she felt like she could see things a little clearer. Her heart was still broken, but this time, when she swallowed, there wasn't unmeasurable pain any longer. As much as there was pain, there was also the presence of peace and knowing she would be ok.

***

On the other side of town, DeVon sat on the bed in his appointed room at Angel and Jay's house. He was in shock to learn of all the things his boy Jay went through as a child. He thought he had it bad, but maybe his little ten years with his parents was something that Jay could have only dreamed of. DeVon was shocked to feel the water filling up in his eyes, and it seemed as if his heart was crying for his boy. His mind was telling him, *be a man, suck it up. Men don't cry and especially not for their boy.* But he couldn't help but feel the pain that Jay lived through as a child and yet still found a reason to smile. In his mind, if there is a God, and there must be for Jay to have lived through that stuff, He owed Jay a solid, and that was why He gave him Angel. He laughed to himself as he thought, "Did God literally take an angel out of heaven and just give it to Jay?" Either way, at least God had Jay's back because He surely did not have his, and it was time to get back to reality.

As DeVon stared at his phone of an old connection he had as a youngster that helped him to take care of Caroline and her baby boy, he had old memories flashing through his mind. He thought to himself, *one push of the button on this name and all my financial burdens will be over. I can make some things happen. Get a car and a place to stay. I bet Destiny would want me back for sure, then. It will be a win for sure. I get to have her back and get that no-good husband back.* The only way to him was through her, and the smell of vengeance flared his nostrils as he made the call that would redirect his life.

Downstairs in the living room, Jay, now sitting alone with his thoughts on the couch, couldn't make sense of those feelings that had come up. He had gotten over the pain of how he was raised and considered himself to be a blessed man living a good life. He was just trying to share with DeVon the power of God and what He could do in his life. He never imagined it would stir up this anger he was now feeling in his heart as he replayed an instance in which, once again, his mother showed him who had the power.

Mother: Boy, get in here right now and clean up this kitchen.

Jay: Yes, mam.

20 minutes later

Mother: (yelling) Jay, if I have to come in there and get you, I will drag you into this kitchen.

Jay: *(running to the kitchen)* I was watching TV. Why can't I clean up when wrestling goes off?

Jay's mother, filled with rage that he would have the audacity to talk back or question her, sent fire up her spine. *This little boy needs to be checked.* And before another word was spoken, the bleach that sat on the counter beside the sink to wash dishes was in her hands and, in a blink, was in Jay's eyes. As Jay cried, screamed, and rubbed his eyes, his mother's suddenly calm voice advised him, "Don't you ever talk back to me, boy. You do what I tell you to do."

Angel walked down the stairs and saw Jay sitting on the couch, massaging his heart. Her discernment instantly realized what was going on. Without saying a word, she sat next to her husband, pulled his large 6'2 muscular framed body into her medium-sized arms, and laid his head on her bosom. Although they were small, they were large enough for him to have a resting place for his head and for his broken heart. Angel and Jay sat quietly as she rubbed his head and allowed him to be broken for the moment, because she knew the spirit within them both would bring him back to peace.

Chapter Six

Life's Marathon

I've run this race; my heart is tired. I've run this race; I want to go higher. I've run this race chasing after you. I ran the race in hopes that you would chase me, too.

I've run this race and peace I have found. I've run this race until I was heaven-bound. I have run this race to your arms, I have run this race until victory is won.

I ran this race from the streets to her arms. I ran this race, and it brought me harm. I ran this race of trying to walk this road. I ran until I decided I would run no more.

***

For whom the Lord loveth he chasteneth, and scourgeth every son whom he receiveth. If ye endure chastening, God dealeth with you as with sons; for what son is he whom the father chasteneth not? (Hebrews 12:6-7, KJV)

The Chase

DeVon pulled into the parking lot of the meet-up spot with Kevo. He got out of the car to greet a man he hadn't seen since his twenties. By the look of it, DeVon was not the only one who aged.

DeVon: My guy, what's shaking, old man?

Kevo: Baby boy, I thought my ears was deceiving me on the phone. I had to pull up, and now my eyes got to be playing tricks on me. The dead have arisen. Some ghosts come to hunt, and some to play. What kind of ghost does my eyes bear witness to today?

DeVon: I see you still got that smooth tongue, man. I see nothing has changed but the date, well, and your weight *(as DeVon popped Kevo on the belly to emphasize the growth around his midsection, the men burst into laughter)*. Man, I need a come-up, and I need it fast. Life out here is life-ing me, and I can't keep up on the good-boy road. I tried. It's not for me. I was hoping you could push some weight my way.

Kevo smiled with the evil grin he had since DeVon could remember. He thought he had lost one of his soldiers to the good-boy life. It only took about 20 years for him to come to his senses. Run-Man, which Kevo affectionately called DeVon in his street days, had come back.

Kevo: Man, you ain't said nothing but a word. Run-Man, jump in the car with me. Let's go for a ride and talk a bit.

DeVon was a bit nervous because he just needed some work. He really didn't want to get a family dynamic started with Satan's side-kick. He knew Kevo was foul. He had been for over 25 years. But he had what could get DeVon/Run-Man back on his feet in these streets.

DeVon: Man, I got some things to do and need to get going. I just need to see if I can lift something off you. I can do a 50/50 on a front.

Kevo: *(grinning and causing DeVon to become very uncomfortable)* I got you. I tell you what. Let's go for a ride and have a talk. I will not only front you the weight, but I can put a little change in your pocket to sustain you. Run-Man can't get back out here in these streets riding this Camry. I heard times was hard for you, guy, but a Camry? *(they both laughed)*.

DeVon: This is my boy's car. I'm using it for right now. But let's go. Just make sure I get back in 20. I have something I have to do *(his mind is eager to return to the scene of the crime)*.

***

*O*n the other side of town:

Destiny stood in her kitchen feeling lost and empty. Chris was a horrible husband, and without him being in the house, she thought she would be happy. Yet, she found herself lonely and feeling as though she had finally made the biggest mistake of her life. Maybe she was wrong about all this. Maybe Zondra was clueing her in on a part of life and giving her some real knowledge and wisdom that she really didn't get growing up. No one talked to her about men and women dynamics. The only marriage she witnessed on a regular basis was her grandparents, and they were the exception to the rule. They never lived this life that she was being forced to live. They were good people. Destiny laughed as she thought to herself, *they sure don't make them like Granddaddy anymore.*

As Destiny entered the closet of the master bedroom, her mind was made up on one thing for sure. She was going to church tomorrow. She may not have known what to do, but she knew where to go to find her peace. It was always her safe place. Her mind flashbacked to a movie she saw on TV while lying on that couch (the story of her life) to a scene where the husband surprised his wife and showed up at church and got saved. They lived happily ever after. She dreamed of that with DeVon. Sure, they had some large hurdles to get over, but she loved that man. Most importantly, she knew he loved her. Right or wrong, the love was real.

Destiny choked on her thoughts of DeVon. She was not sure if the TV could be her point of counseling this time around. There was something in DeVon's eyes at that hospital the last time they spoke. It was as if she didn't recognize him. His body was there, and it was his face, but she knew the eyes of her love. The cornea, iris, and pupil that stared at her were not DeVon's. It was like someone had taken control of his body and mouth and was using him like a ventriloquist.

Destiny, sitting on the floor of her closet, became nauseous that even in the moment of her love being used by the enemy, God was still there with her. He had to be. How else could she have stood firm in her faith against the plan of her heart's desire to fulfill her promise to God for the very spirit that is now screaming and calling her names?

Her reflection on that moment caused her to remember the time she was homeless at eighteen, literally staying with strangers. She had no money, no food, no transportation, no job. And although she had nothing, she never went without. Strangers housed her, fed her, prayed for her, and would send her on her way. On that closet floor, Destiny, for the first time in her life, realized just how blessed she had always been. She was kept by God. She realized she had a hedge of protection that kept her. He never let her go. He consumed her, chased after her, going after her, like the one sheep that went astray, leaving behind the 99. Her head was lifted, and she had turned to Him. She had turned to the one that kept her safe in the lion's den, the one that got down in the fiery furnace with her. How did Destiny know this? When she considered all the hardest moments of her life, she realized she was still standing; she was a little off but still in her right mind. A once homeless woman was now sitting on the floor in the closet of a bedroom that was the size of her entire first apartment.

It all makes sense. He wouldn't allow her to rejoice in her wrongdoings, but He allowed her to survive them, to take another breath and consider how she could have left this earth in sin, never having a moment to repent. He sought her, and now she was determined more than ever to seek Him.

Leaving the house to run to the store, Destiny noticed a familiar car parked down the street from the house. While there were many of these cars all around, she found it odd that the same car that she had watched for weeks while DeVon was in the hospital seemed to be the very same one with a dent on the back driver-side door. Destiny pulled out of the driveway and decided that instead of going right, she would go left. Perhaps it was a coincidence and someone was visiting a neighbor with that same dent.

She slowed down while approaching the car to her left. Her mind began to race, and she wondered, "What is he doing, and what is he doing here?" As she rolled the window down to greet the driver, she realized this was not who she thought it was. She thought…

Destiny: DeVon? Baby, what are you doing? DeVon? Baby, do you hear me?

DeVon stared back but refused to roll the window down; he looked at the woman who changed his life for the better or perhaps for the worse. Finally rolling the window down, he remembered he had to keep a straight face. She was the key to finding Chris.

DeVon: Hey baby, how you doing?

Destiny: *(confused)* I'm good. How are you? What are you doing? Why are you here?

DeVon: *(gets out the car, and bends down to eye level at Destiny's window)* I'm here just looking around. I needed to come back and see this spot for myself. You know, visiting the scene of the crime.

He gave Destiny a smirk that was very weird and unsettling in her spirit. She loved DeVon, but this didn't feel right. There was no humbleness in his voice. Everything within her was saying not to believe or trust what he was saying.

Destiny: Baby, I know you have been through a lot. But you are scaring me. Something isn't right. Where is Jay?

DeVon: *(now yelling)* Scaring you? Did you just say that I am scaring you? This coming from the woman whose husband, on this very street, almost took my life. No, let me take that back. He did take my life. After dealing with you, the only thing I had left was you and my truck, and look at me now. Look at me!

Destiny couldn't stop the tears from flowing. DeVon's rage was not something she was familiar with. The once-loving man who only put his hands on her to love her and his lips to speak life into her was now spilling out as much venom as he could to her. Sadly, she felt like he was right. This was all her fault, just as Chris had described in the driveway the last time she saw him. Everybody's life she entered she screwed up. So, if she couldn't do anything else, she was just going to sit and take it. Maybe if DeVon got it out, he would feel better.

Destiny: Baby, I am so…

DeVon: *(in a weird calmness)* Be careful with that word *baby*.

Destiny: DeVon, I am so sorry for all of this. I screwed up. I have messed everyone's life up. You have to know that I really did love you. Everything I said and did was how I felt. As mad as you are right now, nothing will convince me that you didn't love me the same way.

DeVon's heart was melting. This was the Destiny he fell in love with. This was the humble woman who always had him curious as to her thoughts. It seemed like her heart always spoke for her. He tried his best to stay strong and focus on the plan. *Get to Chris, by any means necessary, get to Chris. Remember who you are now. You are Run-Man, and it's about time for precious Destiny to meet him. Let her know you are not the lame man she thinks you are.*

DeVon: *(game face, come on Run-Man; shoot your shot)* Baby, you are right. I still love you, and I know you love me. Forgive me for talking to you like that. You know you will always be my baby doll.

Destiny: *(drying her tears and hearing her man's voice for the first time in weeks).* I don't know what it will take to fix all of this, but I do know who can fix it. I don't want to lose you. I just want to do things right. Do you want the same, DeVon? Do you still love me?

DeVon: *(silently sarcastic)* Of course, I do. You are the love of my life. My last shot at love.

Destiny, feeling comfortable now, slightly opened the door, and DeVon took a step back so that she could get out of the car. They met face to face, body to body, heart to heart. Destiny placed her hands in DeVon's hands.

Destiny: So, where do we go from here? How do we fix us?

DeVon: Don't you worry your pretty little head. Let me take the lead on this. I got it. You just take care of you. Hey baby, where is Chris? *(Destiny, shocked he would even ask)* I'm just asking because a brother can't take another chance at being shot again.

Destiny: Oh, he moved out. It is over, and he has filed for a divorce.

DeVon: *(anger brewing)* He filed for divorce? Not you?

Destiny: He beat me to the courthouse. I understand the rush of him doing it with all that took place.

DeVon: I don't understand why you didn't rush to do it with all that took place. He shot the man you love. The man you claim you want to spend your life with, and it took him filing.

Destiny: I was at the hospital seeing about you. I had to sit and watch for Angel and Jay to leave, but I was always there day and night. His filing made it easier for me to continue to see about you.

DeVon believed Destiny, but Run-Man didn't. And for the first time since his twenties, he heard those two voices again speaking to him.

Run-Man: Man, don't believe her. This is just straight game. She was hoping that fool would stay, and she will be taken care of.

DeVon: She loves you, man. You felt her presence when she was there. Remember, you couldn't open your eyes, but her tear dropped on your hand, making you realize that you could still feel while you lay there paralyzed.

Run-Man: We need to get rid of that fool once and for all. He has us looking weak out here in these streets. We have a reputation to uphold, man. Look, let's handle the business like we always did. Forget her. It's you and me, baby. We can play all day to get that fool to come our way. You know, ain't nothing ever came to a sleeper but a dream. Let's make something shake.

DeVon laughed a little to himself because surely Run-Man's voice is Kevo-inspired. *But he's right. We're done chasing empty dreams of hope wrapped up in the arms of a woman. We are chasing money and mayhem. That's it, that's all.* DeVon/Run-Man focused back on the conversation with Destiny.

DeVon: You are right. None of this matters. At least it's getting done so we can be together. So, what you got up? What are you about to get into?

Destiny: I am running to the store to get a few things. I am going to finally cook a good meal for tomorrow and go to church.

DeVon: *(rolling his eyes)* Church? Why are you going there?

Destiny: *(confused but understanding)* I am just tired of running from God. I keep trying to fix things myself, and they only get worse. I have realized that not only did He heal you, but He had been there for me throughout my life: the good and the bad.

DeVon: So that's what you on? You, Jay, and Angel reading from the same book of foolery.

Destiny: *(now bothered by DeVon's tone and ready to go, she gets in the car)* DeVon, you may want to consider all you went through and how you have been brought out of it. We were wrong. What we did was wrong, and God still had our backs. I know you are fixated on believing Chris shot you, but he didn't. However, I see I can't convince you otherwise. You will have to see for yourself.

Run-Man: See man! You see how she takes up for that fool.

DeVon: Yeah, you right. I tell you what. Can I get a plate when you leave church tomorrow?

Destiny was confused but relieved that DeVon was trying to come to his senses. It was just going to take a little time. With all he has been through, she just needed to be patient with him. Perhaps it was the pain meds that he was on that had him out of his mind at times.

Destiny: Sure. I will be happy to fix you a plate. Where do you want to meet to get it?

Run-Man: Why we got to get a plate? The fool gone. After all we been through, that is our house now. Why we can't take our shoes off and sit at the table and eat?

DeVon: *(sarcastically kind)* So now he's finally gone, and the house is yours, and I can't get an invite?

Destiny: For now, let's just meet somewhere. I want to do right. And the right thing is to wait 'til the divorce is final and they declare the house is mine. Honestly, I may request we just sell the house in the divorce. *(Looking back at the house)* Besides, it holds too many bad memories at this point.

Run-Man: Boss man, fall back on this. We have got to keep her in a good space so that we can get to Chris. She is our only road to finding him.

DeVon: Ok. I can get with that. Just call me when you get out of church.

DeVon got in his car, and he and Destiny pulled off at the same time, headed in different directions, much like their life right now. As much as they loved one another, they were headed down two different paths.

***

But I see another law in my members, warring against the law of my mind and bringing me into captivity to the law of sin which is in my members. O wretched man that I am! Who shall deliver me from the body of this death? I thank God through Jesus Christ our Lord. So then with the mind I myself serve the law of God; but with the flesh the law of sin. (Romans 7:23-25, KJV)

Chapter Seven

<u>Weapons</u>

The battleground is tough, and we all must go. Showing up for the fight, and it's man to man, soul to soul. You show up alone with empty hands; you will catch your feet slipping in sinking sand.

Training time is done; the moment has arrived. Are you going to fall desolate to the enemy, or will you rise? The fight begins, and it's blow to blow. Is this the moment you reap what you sow?

The war is over; victory has been won. When the dust settles, what side are you standing on?

Weapons/Armor Up

Run-Man had been living it up, just like the good old days. Finally, he had money in his pockets, a new car, and in one more month, he would be ready to move out. His days of staying under Jay and Angel's roof were finally numbered. Just like DeVon, Run-Man thought Jay and Angel were cool people but too holy for him. He loved walking around the house, listening to them talk about their God and making them think he was listening. A lot of the stories they told were funny because they told him what he already knew about them. He was there. He was offended at their accusing him of a lot of things he had nothing to do with. Like the time Jay got shot. He didn't create that scene. That was Jay's choice. But ol' softie DeVon was feeling sorry for him and had to sit and listen. Run-Man was just happy that Jay was too emotional to go into details about it. Those little details could have implicated him in the saga. At the end of the day, people always wanted to accuse him of things that went wrong, but they had a choice. No different than when he approached Eve in the garden. He didn't force her to eat the fruit. She made the decision. All he did was ask the question. By this time, Run-Man was sick of everybody, including DeVon. He was bored now and ready to wage war on anyone he encountered. Anybody and everybody could get it at this point.

Jay came down the stairs to eat dinner and ran into DeVon.

Jay: Hey man, let's eat.

DeVon: Y'all go ahead; I need to run a few errands.

Jay: You have missed dinner every night this week. Is everything ok with you? I know how much you love Angel's food.

DeVon reached into his pants pocket and pulled out a roll of cash so large that it pulled his shirt up and revealed his gun as he tried to get his hand out of his pocket.

DeVon: Everything is everything, man. Oh, by the way, here is something for letting me lay my head here.

Jay: *(in disbelief at what he just saw, pushing the offer of cash away from him)* Your money is no good here, man.

DeVon: I appreciate you guys looking out for me. It shouldn't be much longer. I made an offer on a house, and if all goes well, we will close within the month. You and wifey can have your house back and do what y'all do.

Jay was concerned to the point he could no longer deny it. He had been watching how DeVon was moving lately, and it was questionable. Now he had a roll of cash with no job, and he was ready to move. Again, with no job.

Jay: A house? Man, what do you have going?

DeVon: What you mean?

Jay: Don't play with me, playboy. In one month, you have pulled up to this house with no job and a brand-new BMW. You're shopping for clothes and never wearing the same thing twice. I walked into your room to bring you some more sheets, and you have Jordans and Ferragamos all over the floor. And let me say again, for the record, with no job.

DeVon: Why are you paying that much attention to me?

Jay: Dude, I work 40+ hours a week. I have a three-bedroom, two-bathroom house in which I have an old Camry and an old Maxima sitting in my garage. And you park a brand-new BMW in the driveway every night. Make it make sense.

DeVon: *(laughing)* Awe, man, do you want one? I can get you one.

Jay: Quit playing with me. I keep telling you I wasn't always saved. DeVon, don't tell me you are doing what I think you are doing. And you're coming back to my house where my wife lays her head.

DeVon: Quit tripping, my guy. I am doing what I have to do. I told you, I am done with being broke. I'm done with the fairy tale dream of that so-called righteous life. It's time to do what I know works and what puts money in my pocket.

Jay: "For what shall it profit a man, if he shall gain the whole world, and lose his own soul?"[3] Brother, I have been there. I am telling you that you are in a losing battle. This is not the life you want. You should know that from your past.

DeVon: Here is what I know. I know I was a lonely man, trying to live this good boy life. I had a job, a car, a place to stay, a son, and finally, a woman that I loved. And in a matter of 30 days, I had none of that, plus a bullet in my chest.

Run-Man: That's it, my boy. Tell him! Tell him what it is! He forgot, but you didn't. Teach that fool what loyalty looks like.

DeVon/Run-Man: *(no longer caring what Jay says or thinks)* I'm done taking losses. This is my time to get back everything that fool took from me.

Jay looked at a mask of what appeared to be DeVon's face, but not his eyes, not the spirit he had seen before.

Jay: DeVon, what are you saying?

DeVon/Run-Man: *(Lifting his shirt to display the armor sitting on his side)* I am saying this is what it is; this is what it's gone be. First, I am going to take care of that fool that took my woman and tried to take

---

3   Mark 8:36, KJV

my life. I won't be a coward like him and just walk away and leave him breathing. I am going to make sure the job is done. After that, I am going to go get his wife, my woman, and put her up in my house. I will be back on top with a crib, a couple of cars, a woman, and plenty of money to spend. You see, everything can be brought with a price. Between these dollar signs and this steel, I'm locked and loaded.

Jay was shocked but grounded, refusing to be moved by the enemy he saw in the mask of his boy's eyes. He knew this spirit. He recognized the lust of the flesh, the lust of the eyes, and the pride of life using his friend's face.

Jay: Let me tell you this with clarity and understanding. As for me and my house, we will serve the Lord.

DeVon/Run-Man: *(trying to turn and walk off)* Man, don't nobody want…

Jay heard in his spirit, "Make no friends with a man given to anger, nor go with a wrathful man, lest you learn his ways and entangle yourself in a snare."[4] Jay understood the assignment. He would not be moved by the emotions that were seeping into his heart because he bought DeVon into his home and around his wife. He loved his boy, but if he was going to allow the enemy to take control, he must go. "Fear not, for I am with you; be not dismayed, for I am your God; I will strengthen you, I will help you, I will uphold you with my righteous right hand."[5]

Jay: I tell you what; we are at a crossroads, but my brother, I love you, and this is getting settled tonight. If you have any respect for me, put your ego aside and let me ask you a question, man to man.

DeVon realized he had gone too far and owed Jay more than an answer to his question, so he listened.

DeVon: What's up?

---

4 Proverbs 22:24-25, ESV

5 Isaiah 41:10, KJV

Jay: *(pointing at Jay's gun and pocket of money)* Do you really think that is the answer to it all? That the armor you have is going to bring you happiness and love?

DeVon: At this point, yeah.

Jay: Let me have 20 minutes of your time. I give you my word; after this, you never have to worry about me pushing my faith on you. The truth of the matter is that our Father gives us free will to choose Him. He doesn't force Himself on us, so I dare not force Him on you. But let me just tell you where that piece of armor you have is going to lead you.

As Jay and DeVon sat, Jay was reminded of the armor that almost cost him his life. That was the night that led to his decision to change the armor of death for the Armor of Life.

Jay reflected on the night one of his biggest deals was about to go down that would set him up for life but almost took his life.

Jay: Man, I was seventeen years old and had a home girl. She let me know that someone who was on the block all the time wanted to make some bigger moves and asked if I could spot him. Me being who I have always been, even in the world, I wanted to help the little dude come up. The same way Ray helped me come up when Pumpkin needed clothes for her first day of school. I wanted to return the favor. So, I served the guy a couple of times, even fronted him for some work with no interest in the payback.

By the third round, I had gotten comfortable with him and wasn't concerned when he called for a meet-up. But something was off. I couldn't put my finger on it, but all afternoon, I had this leery feeling I couldn't shake. My sweet Dea' was talking to me as I got ready to go, and she even said she had a bad feeling and asked me to stay home with her and watch some TV. At first, I agreed, but my greed for that drop was bigger than my concern. I ignored her, and I ignored the spirit within me.

When I pulled up to the alley, it wasn't surprising he had his boy with him. I knew these fools, so I wasn't worried. He let me know he wanted more than what he asked for, and I walked back to my car. As I reached down under the driver seat, suddenly *bang, bang, bang, bang, bang*! Heat hit my body instantly as I hit the ground. My body was on fire. This fool stepped over my dying body to get what I had and left me lying there. My mind was in complete disbelief that my life was about to end in an alley on the ground with the smell of urine and garbage filling my nostrils. This was how my life was coming to an end. Luckily, a woman was looking out the window when she heard the shots and called 911.

As I lay in the back of the ambulance, I couldn't take the pain anymore. I had given up. If my life was coming to an end, at least Dea' wouldn't have to see me chalked out on the ground. There was this light that I was floating towards. This light grew brighter and brighter when I heard the lady who was sitting with me yelling, "We are losing him! Clear!" I felt a hit on my chest so hard, it snatched me from that beautiful light back into the back of the ambulance. I get to the hospital, and, of course, they lose me again. I woke up in pain, and the doctor told me that I had been shot five times. They were having trouble regulating me and found there was another bullet in me, and they rushed me down for emergency surgery. I recall a nurse telling the doctor they couldn't do the surgery without my mother's permission and the doctor saying he didn't care; they were taking me before I died.

I lived through it, came out with my street cred and a bullet still lounged in the chamber of my heart to this day. My dad came into town and saw about me. Got my medicine, bought me a hat, a coat, and a gun, and that was the last time I ever laid eyes on him. The anger from him leaving, the anger from what I had gone through just trying to eat and make sure my family ate as kids, and most of all, for what those fools had done filled me up with hatred. I was about that life, and I was ready for vengeance. I smelled those boys' blood in my nostrils. They had to go.

Dea' knew what was brewing in my heart. That woman was full of wisdom. She was sitting with me on the couch during my recovery, and I guess she knew what was on my mind, and she said, "Baby, don't fatten frogs for snakes." *(DeVon looked confused at the phrase, and Jay laughed)* I know, man. That was my look, too. But what she meant was don't give the devil more fuel for the fire. The crazy part is that no matter what she said, my mind was made up. I wanted them, but by the time I was up and back out in those streets, they were nowhere to be found. I didn't care; there was no rock I was leaving unturned.

I eventually ran into one of their old knockoffs and thought that if I played on her, she would tell me where they were or at least the one that pulled the trigger. Instead, she told me about God and how He had changed her life, and she was going to school for her degree and working. I just thought it was a bunch of talk and didn't care. But I let her talk. Eventually, she would give in on at least one of the two things I had decided I wanted from her. Either him or her, if you know what I mean. After a while, I not only started believing she was for real, but her conversations gave me so much peace. I found myself enjoying just talking with her and asking her questions about her faith. Man, I even went to church with her.

A year of teachings at church, videos she would send of sermons, us being on the phone, and her reading scriptures from the Bible to me had me feeling some type of way. One day, she had to work late, and that was the night she normally read to me. I texted her and told her that I was really looking forward to her finishing the chapter she was reading because I wanted to know what happened. She told me to read it for myself. I told her I didn't have a Bible. She told me to Google it *(laughing)*. I did because I was bored waiting for her to get off work and call me. Let's just say I haven't stopped reading since.

You know those disciples were just as gangster as we were. One named Peter, who walked with Jesus, chopped a man's ear off. Right in front of Jesus because he was being disrespectful. I couldn't believe it, but those guys in the Bible was no different from us. At least, that is how I felt. But what finally got me was my guy, Paul. Paul was going around arresting people for teaching the name of Jesus until he had an encounter with God himself. He went from arresting them to being one of them. His belief was so strong that he then sat in the very jail that he put others in. While in there, he wrote letters telling them just how real God was and all the stories had been true. It's like he was foreseeing a war that was not in the physical but in the spiritual realm. And even in that type of war, you got to have your Armor.

He tells the people, "Be strong in the Lord, and in the power of his might. Put on the whole armor of God, that ye may be able to stand against the wiles of the devil. For we wrestle not against flesh and blood, but against principalities, against powers, against the rulers of the darkness of this world, against spiritual wickedness in high places. Wherefore, take unto you the whole armor of God, that ye may be able to withstand in the evil day, and having done all, to stand." [6]

This blew my mind. I realized at that moment I was at war with me. *(DeVon looking confused but interested)*. The fight was bigger than me and the guy I was looking for. It was against the principalities that we can't see with our natural eye. It was against what I wrestled with within. Before dating this young lady, there was no wrestling because there was only one spirit that existed within me. That was the sin that I was born into and the iniquities of this world that I was shaped into. That was always present. However, once she introduced me to the word of God and I began to listen to some of her readings, there was a pull that made me desire to listen. This pull was something else in me

---

6   Ephesians 6:10-13, KJV

that was now in constant battle with the other. Using her to find this man so that I could put my hands on him was fine initially. But through listening, I became very uncomfortable with using her. Not only that, but my mind was no longer consumed with finding him. Don't get me wrong. I still wanted him. But it wasn't my daily thought process any longer. I realized I was in a fight. I was fighting within me against me. Within me against him, and he was doing the same within himself. We are all being deceived by the enemy to fight one another so that we are not fighting against him. He comes to kill, steal, and destroy us. I thought my reputation was at stake, not considering my soul for eternal life was at stake.

So, I continued reading, and Paul tells us what we need to battle. You need the full armor of God. He starts with having your loins girt about with truth, the breastplate of righteousness, feet walking in the peace of the gospel, the shield of faith, the helmet of salvation, and the sword of the word of God. And praying with prayer and supplication in the Spirit. [7]

DeVon: See right there, man. I was with you until you started talking about loins and girt. What does that even mean?

Jay: (*grateful that DeVon even asked*) Hear me out, my brother. It may even sound like an attack on you. I promise it's not. It is an attack on what is operating within you. But it will make you upset. So, let's break this down. The first thing Paul said is, "having your loins girt about with truth." Loins is the place in your body on either side of your backbone that is below your rib cage and above your hipbone. One can say it is the waist area that also encompasses the private part of the human body that detects the difference between man and wom-an—so, having your loins girt about with truth. Girt means belted or wrapped. If you put on a belt, the belt is worn around you. It is a circle

---

7 Ephesians 6:10-18, KJV.

from front to back, side to side. Girt is to surround, encircle, enclose, or encompass your waist area with truth. What is truth as it relates to the Bible? It is the word of God. There are many *(hand quotations)* truths in the world; it may be your truth but not my truth. However, anything pertaining to God, it is the word that we stand on. That is our law in the land of the living.

So, He wants me to surround my waist with truth. I wrestled with that understanding for the longest. And why is it the first thing we put on? You must consider the belt is the centerpiece that binds your clothes together. It is considered the tool used to hold everything else up. But it still bothered me, and here is where it may be hard for you, my brother, as it was me. I realized one of the enemies' greatest deceptions was the sexual immorality of God's people. We love being together and with one another in the bedroom. We look at it as just some form of connection to the other person without understanding the depth of the connection. It is spirit-exchanging. When you lay with a woman, and she receives you, she receives every spirit that is operating within you. Have you ever wondered why you were so tired once you reached the peak of the moment? It is because you lose strength. You are drained because you lost a part of you, and she just gained a part of you that she now carries.

The word, which is "the truth," says that we should restrain from fornication unless we have taken on a wife. "For this is the will of God, even your sanctification, that ye should abstain from fornication." [8] When you lay with your chosen wife, she is there to give back to you that in which you have given her. So, you never lose yourself; you only multiply because a woman takes a seed and causes it to grow. Her assignment for your life is clear to her, and through prayer, she can take what you have given her physically and spiritually and multiply it. I don't care how good a woman is. You cannot get the fullness of favor

---

8   1 Thessalonians 4:3, KJV.

from God unless she is your wife. So here is the lesson to girt about your loins with truth. When you get out of bed, you can get out of your head about the cloudy decisions you make in this life.

DeVon: I'm still not convinced, but I am interested; go on.

Jay: Once you have your loins girt about with truth, then you can seek God for a clean and righteous heart. Jeremiah talks about how deceitful the heart is above all things, and it is wicked. [9] I couldn't understand how people say follow your heart when the heart is deceitful. Did you know all the blood in your body flows through your heart?

(DeVon sat up now, listening intensively).

Well, it is the same in the spiritual realm. All spirits flow through our heart. Now, if we were born in sin automatically and shaped in our iniquities, what type of spirit do you think is flowing through our hearts? It is only when we accept Jesus as our Lord and Savior that we are born again. Reading His Word concerning our lives replaces the deceitful heart with a righteous heart. It is only through Christ Jesus that we can have this. What you feed is what will grow. When you feed your body the Word, the spirit man will grow. You feed your body the world, and your flesh will grow. Once you have read the word of God, repented, and prayed, you can then ask God our Father for the breastplate of righteousness.

Now, here is where I think we are attacked the most by the enemy other than our loins. Our minds…. Our minds are one of the most powerful tools we have in our bodies. In the flesh, it is our minds that cause us to think and tell our bodies what to do every single day. Think about this, DeVon. A person can have a strong heartbeat. But if he is considered brain dead, physically, they call him a vegetable and say he should be pulled off a machine. It is because the brain is not able to tell the body to breathe. Like so, if you are brain dead to the instructions

---

9   Jeremiah 17:9, KJV.

of our Father, you are literally walking around gaining the world and yet losing your life. A strong mind incorporates the fruits of the spirit. [10] A strong mind is disciplined to self-control; it causes you to have patience with people, love for your fellowman, kindness, and faithfulness to others, especially your wife. The way I am being with you as we speak. Most of all, love. However, when your mind is filled with all the foolishness of this world, and you're preoccupied with thoughts of revenge, anger, frustration, and greed, you can't think clearly. Your decisions become dangerous.

So, how do you prevent this? By asking God for one sound mind. By stating to Him what is already in His Word, let the mind that was in Christ Jesus also be in me. [11] No matter what I may face, to be about my Father's business until the end of my life in this earth. At that point, you can ask for the helmet of salvation. This helmet will produce for you the fruits of the spirit.

With the shield of faith, Paul says you can destroy all the weapons that the enemy throws at you. In my opinion, this simply means my faith is rooted in God's word that He will NEVER leave me nor forsake me, that He shall cover me with his feathers, and under his wings shalt I trust: his truth shall be my shield and buckler. So, I don't have to be afraid of the terror by night nor the arrows that fly by day. I don't fear the pestilence that walks in darkness nor the destruction at day. A thousand can fall at my side and ten thousand at my right hand, but it will not come near me. I will only witness with my eyes the reward of the wicked. Because my Lord is my refuge, and he will send his angels to keep me in all my ways. [12] Because of this promise of truth in His Word and the inventory that I can look back on over my life and see

---

10   Galatians 5:22-23

11   Philippians 2:5

12   Psalms 91:4-11

what He has brought me from and delivered me from sharpens my shield of faith. It allows me to speak in the earth with boldness and clarity.

But I would not be able to feel this way and know these things if it had not been for His Word. His Word is my sword in the spiritual fight. Your gun in the physical is His word for me. I get it that society has sold the faith on emotions, that we don't understand that it doesn't matter how we feel as much as we need to know what He says. His spoken word will cause demons to run. Even when Jesus, the perfect one who came to pay the price for the redemption of our sins, was tempted, His only strike against the enemy was the words, "It is written." [13] All He needed was the Word, and in each attempt, He was able to give the enemy a word against the very thing He was tempted with. My brother, if you were ever confused about life, as I assume you to be right now, for every situation, there is a word from God on how to deal with it in that book *(as he pointed to his well-worn Bible that sat at on the coffee table)*. You're angry, and you want revenge; it's there. You're sick of heartache and pain; it's there. You want a wife; it's there. You want to know how to be a husband; it's there. Dealing with authority, being the one in authority. It is all in the pages of this book we call the Bible.

Lastly, my brother, to complete your armor of God, the only other thing you need is to walk in the gospel of peace. With everyone, you walk in peace according to the word of God *(he picked up the bible to show DeVon)*. All that you need to be in this earth and to interact with others is right here. But you want to know what is also in these pages? Words of expression from witnesses who walked with His Son here on earth before His crucifixion. The stories they shared of His patience and love and His message from the Father, our creator, for us. The message from the very one who knew us before He formed us in

---

13   Matthew 4:1-11, KJV

our mother's womb. [14] He loved us so much that He wanted to make sure centuries ago that we knew how much He loved us and that it was documented for us. All you have to do after accepting Jesus as your Lord and Savior is open your heart, ask the holy spirit for clarity and comprehension, and read.

DeVon felt like he just had an encounter that he couldn't explain, as if, for a moment in time, the world stopped for this conversation. He was compelled and could not deny the words he heard. His heart received every word as truth. He couldn't deny the presence he felt in that room. There must be a spiritual realm, and there had to be a very strong presence of spirit with them that was of peace and love.

DeVon: Hey man, where can I get one of those books?

Jay: Do you accept Jesus Christ as your Lord and Savior, my brother?

DeVon: I'm not sure.

Jay: I tell you what, I have an extra Bible upstairs you can have. I just ask one thing. Before you open it, you pray and ask God for forgiveness for your sins, and you ask God to help you see and give you wisdom and understanding before you open that book.

DeVon: That I can do. As a man, I give you my word.

Jay: Great man; so look, I love you. You are my and Angel's brother, and you will always be, but my brother, you have got to go. I am accountable for this household and that woman in the kitchen. I will not allow anything that I know is against the will of my Father to be present and not stand on it.

DeVon: Hey brother, say no more. After listening to what you just said, I knew that was inevitable. I must admit I respect it. You truly stand for something. But before I go, I got one question I need to know, and I didn't want to interrupt you while you were preaching.

---

14   Jeremiah 1:5

Jay: What's that?

DeVon: What ever happened to that chick that got you into the Word and off that man's a…I mean tail.

Jay: *(smiled as he looked toward the kitchen)* She's in there washing the dishes.

DeVon: *(Shocked)* That was Angel? Angel was once not an angel? What, are you serious?

Jay: I keep trying to tell you, man, we all have a story. Your walk is no different, except that we accepted Jesus as our Lord and Savior and refused to turn back. If you ever meet a person who doesn't have a story of God's great deliverance and forgiveness, if they never talk about the thankfulness for His grace and mercy, you have just met a wolf in sheep's clothing, and you better run.

Both men burst out in laughter as they went into the kitchen to sit for dinner together one last time at the table.

Chapter Eight

Decisions/You Must Decide

DeVon thought long and hard about his conversation with Jay while driving to Destiny's house. He had to be honest with himself, knowing that during their talk, there was a presence of conviction in his heart and mind, but with peace and love, he received it. He couldn't make sense of how it made him feel. His heart drew him to desire more, but his mind was doubtful of it all.

DeVon: *(thinking to himself)* If this life is not for me, this salvation that Jay speaks of, if it's only for people like him, then why do I feel it so strong?

Run-Man: *(speaking to DeVon)* Man, don't believe all that hype. If all that was true, why he let your parents die? Your grandma gone. That fool that took Carolyn and Lil Man from us. He let you lose your job and our crib and car. He's even trying to take Destiny from us. He doesn't care about you. That's for those other folks. Me and you, we got a good thing going. Don't ruin it like you did that time we had to "sit down" for a little while after we shot that buster for being at Carolyn's apartment.

DeVon also hears the words Jay shared that the Father said. *I knew you before I formed you and placed you in your mother's womb. A plate of righteousness and the sword of the word. Girt about your loins with truth.*

As DeVon pulled up to Destiny's house, his heart was heavy, and his mind was busy. He thought to himself, *Perhaps I should talk to Destiny about this.* The last time they talked, she spoke the same game as Jay. It seemed as if they were reading from the same book of "force DeVon to accept someone that didn't accept him."

What DeVon didn't know was how much Destiny had changed. In the past month, she had kept her commitment to return to church and rededicate her life to Christ. Through much prayer and ministry, she was no longer the same person that she was when she last encountered Chris, and "Des" was now silenced.

DeVon rang the doorbell. When Destiny opened the door, she opened DeVon's heart. He was weak for her. All that had happened, and his love still hadn't changed; maybe his respect, but not his love.

Destiny: *(shocked)* DeVon, what are you doing here?

DeVon: What do you mean? I came to see you. Are you going to leave me standing out here talking through a glass door?

Destiny: *(opening the door to step out and talk with DeVon)* DeVon, I am so happy to see you, but I don't want to see you here.

DeVon: Why? What's the problem? Y'all are getting a divorce, or are you lying about that, Destiny?

Destiny: DeVon, calm down. It is not a lie. But…

DeVon: So, what's the problem with me coming in?

Destiny: It's about order, baby. I was serious with you. I have dedicated my life back to Christ. I can't go on with this world the way I was. It's just too hard. I begged Him to save your life. I didn't ask for anything for myself. Only for Him to save you, and He did. Look at you. You are here and in your right mind. To God be the glory for the things He has done.

DeVon was drained. He was tired of fighting with everyone about this man they claimed saved him.

DeVon: Baby, what is going on? Everyone is talking about this God who saved my life, but He was the one who took it. I lost everything, and all He spared was my life. It's easy for you and Jay to believe so strongly in Him when you both can do it from your home. You can get in your car and take a ride. You go to work and get a check; you don't have to look over your shoulder. It's so easy to pray to a God when you're just thanking Him for all He is doing for you.

Destiny: Ah, baby, you couldn't be more wrong. Do you have a moment?

DeVon: *(looking confused and sizing her up)* A moment for what?

Destiny: *(chuckled)* Not that, silly. Can you pull your car out the driveway?

Run-Man: See, man, she about to popcorn on you. Make you look like a buster. You can't even park in the driveway.

Destiny: Park in front of the house, and I am going to grab my purse and pull out of the garage. You can jump in the car with me.

DeVon was so excited to know that they were about to spend time together and that he could leave his car parked that he immediately agreed and ran to his car. A minute later, Destiny pulled out, and DeVon jumped in the passenger seat. The smell of the car brought back memories of the good times they shared, but the sound coming out of the speakers was unfamiliar.

DeVon: What is that you're playing, baby?

Destiny: Oh, it's my worship music. I listen to it coming home from work. It helps me to wind down and get back to a peaceful place.

Run-Man: Here we go again. Why can't she just put on some Maxwell and chill?

DeVon: You know Maxwell can make you chill, too. Ease your mind. Remember how we used to just ride to him?

Destiny: This music is cool, too. Just listen to the words.

Destiny turns the sound up so DeVon can hear clearly. The sounds of Yolanda Adams' voice came through the speaker through a song called "Open My Heart." [15]

DeVon took a moment to swallow the emotions of the words from

---

15   https://youtu.be/W14TybyUfu0.

this song. If ever there was a person in his head who heard his feelings, it was this lady singing his thoughts to him. Someone does understand. Destiny allowed them to continue to ride in silence, for she knew the presence of what she was feeling in the air. It was the spirit of the Most High ministering to DeVon at that moment, and she dared not interrupt.

DeVon looked out the window to hide the heartfelt tears that flowed down the side of his face. For the first time ever, he noticed how green and beautiful the trees were. The wind coming through the sunroof gave him the oxygen he needed to breathe. He had never paid attention long enough to see how beautiful the creation of the earth was. He noticed the body of water as they turned off the road when his thoughts were interrupted by an angelic voice.

Destiny: We are here.

DeVon: Sitting up and looking around. Where are we?

Destiny: My place of peace and sanity.

DeVon was confused but followed Destiny's lead by getting out of the car.

DeVon: I have been in this city my entire life and never knew this was here. This is nice.

Destiny: Most people don't. But this is the place I call Jehovah-Shalom.

DeVon gave Destiny a weird look as they took a seat on a log, seemingly made for two, facing the water.

DeVon: Ja-who? I didn't know you were Jehovah's Witness. You be knocking on people's doors?

Destiny: *(laughing deeply)* Boy, no! It means *the Lord is Peace.* It's the place I found peace during several life-changing moments. I come here. I meditate. I look at the water. *(DeVon turning to Destiny and listening intensely to her)* The first time I came here, I was about 19. I had been going through a lot of heartache and pain trying to find love. I had just been hit with a "Let's just be friends" speech. I was so emotional while driving, I pulled off the road because my tears were blinding me, and I ended up here. I got out of the car and just sat for hours. I never said a word. I didn't call anyone. I didn't even pray. I just sat in my thoughts. The second time I found myself driving here was when I was reflecting on my dad and how I missed a man that I barely knew. My heart ached for him. Through pain, anger filled my heart because I felt that I was cursed in life because of the circumstances that I was born under.

DeVon was even more confused because he hadn't heard this before. While DeVon expressed to Destiny his past pain of his parents, he realized he never asked about hers. He just knew that her father wasn't present in her life, and she left it at that. It's crazy how you can share your story of pain with someone, and they only listen to console you, never sharing their own. He really wanted to know what she meant, but he refused to interrupt her.

And while there were several other times, the last time was while you were in the hospital. I found myself in a situation in which I couldn't even come and care for the man I loved. The circumstances—no, let me call a spade a spade—the decisions that I made had me dealing with consequences I didn't see coming nor could I control.

The decision to commit adultery was dangerous. It didn't seem that way at first. We were two people just wanting love. But it took so much from both of us and almost took your life. Seeing you in that bed, hooked up to a machine to breathe for you, and I wasn't even sure if I was the one who should be praying for you.

What do you do when it's out of your hands? How do you deal with what you can't control? So, this place, Jehovah-Shalom, gives me peace. I speak to God; I repent for my wrongdoing and for going against His instructions for my life. I know in my heart He hears me.

DeVon: How do you know if it goes against His instructions for you? Does He fix it that fast when you talk to Him?

Destiny: Anything that goes against what He has stated in His Word goes against His instructions for our lives. He says thou shall not commit adultery. He didn't tell me I could if my husband was mistreating me. So, our relationship with one another, regardless of how we feel for each other, was not of God's will. Perhaps it was the timing of it all. I knew my marriage was past being on life support. It was dead, and I just refused to bury it. However, as wonderful as it was to have you, it was not in God's divine order, and He cannot bless what He has not given.

The problems were still very present when I got back in my car. I left with the same issues I pulled up with. The difference is that my mind was at peace. My faith helps me to believe that I have turned it over to Him so He will take care of it, me, and everyone involved.

DeVon: But what sense does that make if the problem is not fixed?

Destiny: That's the problem. We are distracted by the enemy trying to fix our own problems. We will have problems 'till the day we leave this earth. Issues will always revolt against us. But what I am learning is that if we are so busy trying to fix it ourselves, we really leave no room for our faith to grow in trusting God to fix it. Plus, it takes away time to sit with Him and to worship Him and get instructions from Him who can fix all things. Hold on, let me get my phone.

Destiny ran to the car to grab her phone. While grabbing it, she inwardly prayed, "Heavenly Father, thank you for this opportunity to be a witness to who you are and your love for us. Please, God, give me the words that I may lift you up, and as I lift you up, you draw his heart unto you. You are God, and only you can change the heart of man. In Jesus' name, I pray, Amen." Destiny sat back next to DeVon, and she pulled up the Holy Bible app on her phone to Matthew 6:30.

Destiny: This is one of the verses that helps me keep my mind at peace with the craziness going on and how to fix it. Are you ok with me reading it to you?

DeVon: *(interested)* Go for it. Let me hear what God is talking about.

Destiny: "Wherefore, if God so clothe the grass of the field, which today is, and tomorrow is cast into the oven, shall he not much more clothe you, o ye of little faith? Therefore, take no thought, saying, what shall we eat? What shall we drink? Or wherewithal shall we be clothed? For your heavenly Father knoweth that ye have need of all these things." Now listen to this part: "But seek ye first the kingdom of God, and his righteousness; and all these things shall be added unto you. Take therefore no thought for the morrow: for the morrow shall take thought for the things of itself." [16]

So, what I got from this was that I am so busy worrying about my life and what will happen. What I want or need to happen. I never considered what he, my creator, wants for me or has designed for me.

DeVon: But why do you think He is your creator and that He has designed something for you? I am here because my momma and daddy got busy and created me.

Destiny: See right there. Such a small but huge trick of the enemy. He wants you to think that is the way life comes to be. Two people just happen to lie down, and from that, scientifically, a baby is born. But guess what? Listen to this… "Before I formed thee in the belly, I knew thee; and before thou camest forth out of the womb I sanctified thee, and I ordained thee a prophet unto the nations." [17]

And then here is my last one, I promise.

Anxiously, Destiny continued to find Scripture to prove her God to DeVon. As DeVon listened intensely to a woman who was teaching him something he refused to learn on his own, he admitted that not only was he shocked about how much she knew, but it also made him look at her with admiration. She wasn't just a pretty face and someone easy to talk to. Her belief was making him consider believing.

---

16   Matthew 6:30-34, KJV

17   Jeremiah 1:5, KJV

DeVon: Go ahead, you are good.

Destiny: "For I know the thoughts that I think toward you, saith the Lord, thoughts of peace, and not of evil, to give you an expected end." [18]

We have always been God's concern. He has always loved us and had a plan for us. Over the years, the enemy has slid into our hearts and our minds with things that are not of our Father, and it has distracted us from seeking Him. And while we are trying to figure it out, the enemy has been running havoc in our homes, families, our hearts, and most of all, our minds. It's almost like we are the hamster in the cage on the wheel that just keeps going and going, but we never get anywhere.

DeVon: I hear you. It sounds real enough. What you reading kind of sounds like what Jay was reading out his Bible. What are you reading from?

Destiny: *(chuckles)* The Bible.

DeVon: *(looking confused)* What?

Destiny: It's an app on my phone. I have a Bible at home that I read during my study time. But this way, I always have the word with me to read and meditate on. Give me your phone.

DeVon handed it over. Destiny still had that power over him; whatever she says goes. Although Chris was still at the forefront of Run-Man's mind, Destiny was the only one on DeVon's mind. She could have access to whatever he had at any given moment. Even the little knock-offs Run-Man had accumulated in the last couple of weeks had nothing on Destiny. In fact, Run-Man might be getting served an eviction notice because Destiny just felt right.

Run-Man: (conversating with DeVon in his head) Say what now, fool? Are you crazy?

DeVon: Watch yourself!

Run-Man: Don't tell me you are falling weak for this girl again.

____

18   Jeremiah 29:11, KJV

Look what she did to us the last time. She almost got us killed. Remember, man, we got a plan. We got to execute the plan. Why don't you smell that vengeance anymore?

Destiny: *(interrupting the fight between the two)* Ok, baby, look, I just downloaded it on your phone. So, if you ever want to hear what God says about you, pray first and then click on the app and start reading.

DeVon: I don't know how to pray.

Run-Man: What is going on? Man, you don't need to know. Shut her up. You are the man. She can't teach you nothing but how to...

Destiny: It's just you talking with God but being honest with Him. Giving recognition to who He is as the creator of everything good and perfect. Tell Him how you feel. It will come to you, I promise. Do you want to talk to Him now?

Destiny grabbed DeVon's hands and closed her eyes. DeVon followed suit and closed his eyes.

Run-Man: Wait! Noooo, wait! I want to...

Destiny: Dear Heavenly Father, I come to you at this moment first to say thank you. Thank you for this opportunity to witness to DeVon of your love and your intention for our lives. Thank you for giving him another chance at life and at getting to know you. Dear God, his mind is confused, but his ears are open. I ask that you continue to open his heart. I ask that you allow people to come into his life and minister to him until he comes running to you, asking, "What must I do to be saved?" I pray the blood of Jesus over his mind. That he begins to seek you. I pray that you speak to him until his heart can no longer deny that you are God. I pray that he will accept you as his Lord and Savior and forever declare your name in the earth. It is in Jesus' name, I pray. Amen.

Destiny opened her eyes to see DeVon's filled with tears that could not be controlled. She didn't say a word. She sat in silence, holding his hand, looking at the water, and allowing God to minister to his heart. DeVon didn't say a word. His heart was full of a feeling he had never felt before. At that moment, it was not about his love for Destiny; it was not about the pain of losing his parents; he couldn't care less about the revenge on Chris. There was a sweet feeling in his heart that was flowing throughout his body in an undeniable way. Words would do it no justice, so he sat in it.

Chapter Nine

Life-Death/Both

A month passed since that day at Jehovah Shalom. DeVon sat on the couch in his new house in silence. He and Run-Man hustled hard in the streets to get everything DeVon thought Destiny would want in a house. And that was all it felt like at this point, just a building, because this couldn't be what "home" felt like. He walked through the beautifully decorated kitchen, choked by the pain of Destiny's decision once again to not even see the place. Run-Man convinced DeVon that Destiny couldn't have loved him if she was willing to walk away from what they worked so hard to get for her. All the fun girls would beg to be there just for a night, and she wouldn't even step foot in what was hers.

He glanced at the Bible she gave him one evening when they met for dinner. As he got up and grabbed it, he flipped through the pages to see all her handwritten sticky notes of thoughts she had on certain scriptures she had read. It seemed to him that all she ever wanted to talk about was God. Truthfully, he enjoyed most of the conversation except for when Run-Man would interfere and try to convince him to get her mind on pleasing him physically instead of talking. Most times, he would force DeVon just to leave her standing in parking lots or the park and pull off, since it was always a "no" from her.

Even more crazy, DeVon had been sharing with Jay all the Scriptures that Destiny had been sharing with him. Now, whenever he saw Jay, he asked about her and how she was doing, even offering that if she needed anything, she could call Angel. The very thing DeVon wished for in the past was now happening. Everybody suddenly accepted Destiny. Well, everyone but Run-Man. Run-Man was the reason he could provide for her if she would just accept it, but the two of them refused to deal with each other. DeVon was beginning to wonder if Run-Man was worth all of this. He now must always look over his shoulder. He couldn't drive anywhere and see the police without becoming spooked. He was always feeling like his next deal was going to be the one that took him out. And now, more than anything, Destiny.

Destiny was not up for negotiation. Destiny had friend-zoned DeVon, and he hated it. He didn't want to be her friend. He wanted to be everything she needed in a man. Her hugs always reminded him of where he was supposed to be. But her *no's* stung like piercings in his heart. She held her relationship with God higher than her feelings for him. Truthfully, DeVon respected it. It felt good to see Destiny walking in her moral values and integrity. He never thought she could be more woman than she was a year ago. But here she was, shining like a diamond he was not worthy of having. She was like one of those virtuous women she read about to him one night on the phone.

DeVon: *(speaking out loud to Run-Man)* Man, you know what? It ain't worth it. Having all of this and sitting here lonely, for what?

Run-Man: *(rolling his eyes in DeVon's head) Man you got to snap out of this. You getting on my nerves. Just call that honey we met last week at the concert.*

DeVon: I don't want her. Nothing about her intrigues me. I liked to be intrigued. You should know that by now. Or is it that you really don't know me at all?

Run-Man: *(with an evil laugh) Look around you, boy. I know you all too well. Look where we are. Look how we got here. Yeah, you are exactly who I told him you were.*

DeVon: *(confused)* Told who? What are you talking about?

Run-Man: Forget all that, man. I am just saying…

Hearing Run-Man triggered a flashback in DeVon's mind. Run-Man's voice was there when he was little and enraged when he saw his parents in their caskets. He remembered that voice when he was upset that his grandmother lied about not being hungry so that DeVon would eat the only food they had. He remembered that voice saying he could go make money for them to have food. And he remembered him being there when he shot the guy Carolyn had started dating. He thought to himself, *why is he always around for these obnoxious moments of life? Steering me to do something opposite of what he had been reading in that Bible lately.*

He suddenly remembered that during those times, he wasn't reading the Bible, nor did he understand the faith enough to believe. He remembered Jay saying how he was out in the streets but had come to know God. And Destiny was having an affair with him, but she had not been the same since reading this same Word. When he thought about it, every time he read the Word, Run-Man was nowhere around. For the first time, he felt used. Jay said something about how the fight was not against each other, but it was within. His heart was filling up again as it had done the day at the "Lake of Peace." Without thought, he picked up the phone.

DeVon: (after 2nd ring, Jay's voice answers) Hey, Jay, I need you, man. I mean, I need God. Something is pulling me, and I don't know what to do. But I don't want to let go. What do I do?

Jay instantly dropped what he was doing. He knew what was happening; he grabbed his keys from the table and got in the car.

Jay: It's ok. Don't let go of it. I am going to stay on the phone. Where are you?

DeVon: I'm at the house.

Jay: Ok, stay on the phone with me, but drop your location.

DeVon: *(drops his location)* Man, I feel like I can't breathe. I feel like I am getting too emotional.

Jay: I am ten minutes from you. It's okay; those emotions are a good thing. Trust me, it is in this moment. Did something happen?

DeVon: I just started thinking about everything. Especially this voice I keep hearing in my head.

Jay: *(showing concern)* What voice are you hearing? What is it saying?

DeVon: It's the voice that talked me into getting back in the game. The one that helps me handle business when I can't seem to get the courage to do it on my own.

Jay: I'm outside; come to the door.

Jay texted Angel to pray immediately, and he said a silent prayer before getting out of the car. *"Father God, it is in the name of Jesus alone that I can, with confidence, come to you. The enemy has risen his head in the life of my brother, DeVon, but you have risen with all power in your hands. You have my whole heart, my whole being, and I give you complete control of me. Father, use me for your will. Father, dispatch your angels to guard and protect us. Let your word come forth like the living water you are. There is no other help I know. No other help I desire and no other help I need. Call DeVon into your marvelous light, dear God. Have your way. It is in Jesus' name, I pray. Amen."*

Run-Man couldn't help but show himself, as he was livid, wanting to know why Jay was there. As Jay walked in the door, he looked at DeVon, and he looked like the face of many, but it was only DeVon. There was a heaviness in the air and a stench. DeVon led him to his formal sitting room. Embarrassed and barely able to look Jay in the eyes, DeVon began to explain this feeling he was having as the two of them sat.

DeVon: Man, I don't know what is going on.

Jay: Tell me what you are feeling, and we will go from there.

DeVon: *(moving his head in motion as if he is scamming the room.)* Is all this worth it? I got everything I desired, yet I feel like I have nothing. I got back in these streets and hustled hard. I am better off than I was before, and I am miserable. This huge house is empty, as if there is no life in it at all.

(Run-Man said to himself within DeVon, "What is this fool talking about? I am giving him everything he wants.")

I miss Destiny like crazy. We talk on the phone, and she always wants to read the Bible together. But she refuses to come over. I have exceeded what that fool Chris did for her, and she doesn't want it. I don't know what else to do. And if I was honest, for some reason, this feeling I am having is not about her. I can't believe I can have all of this and still feel empty inside. I feel dead.

Jay: There is nothing for you to do, my brother, but be patient. If it is God's will, He will bring you together. If I were honest with you, right now, your waiting will be in vain. It sounds to me like Destiny has rededicated her life to Christ, and she is sticking to it. I have a new-found respect for the woman, to be honest *(as he chuckles and realizes that DeVon is not sharing in the laughter).* Seriously, the Word says you will know a tree by the fruit it bears. [19] Regardless of what she did in her past, just as Angel and I did, her fruit shows she belongs to our Father. To your Father. So, my brother, you can offer her the world, but if it comes at the cost of her relationship with God and her soul, you have offered her nothing. You know, I must admit, it shows the beauty of who she was even in her sin. You really had nothing to offer her but time, yet she loved you to the point of almost losing her soul. Now you have money, cars, and all the things this so-called world says

---

19   Matthew 7:16, KJV

you should want, and she wants none of it. I guess the girl was really looking for love the whole time. Just lost and confused by the tricks of the enemy. Now we have you, and you have gained all this stuff, and the only thing you want is her. And she ain't having you unless you have Jesus. That girl sounds Proverbs 31*ish,* after all. I am going to have to repent for the thoughts I used to have regarding her.

DeVon looked upset and confused all at the same time. Some of it made sense, but most of it flew over his head. In his honesty, as Destiny said to just be when it comes to God, he decided to tell Jay how he felt.

DeVon: You see that, man. The way you all feel and talk about God is so far from what I am feeling. But something is tugging at me, and I don't know what to do with it. When I am listening to both of you, I feel at peace. I feel relaxed and even hopeful. But as soon as I leave you all's presence, I am right back to where I originally was and this man talking in my head.

Jay: Let me ask you a question, and just be honest. Do you believe in God?

DeVon: *(thinking hard because he wants to be honest)* Yes, I do. I believe in y'all God. I believe He loves you all.

Jay: Do you believe He loves you?

DeVon: I can't say I do. Look at my life. With all this stuff, I feel as lonely as I did when my grandmother left this earth.

Jay: Do you only listen to us talk about God and only read your Bible when you are with Destiny?

DeVon: Yeah.

Jay: And there you have it, my brother—the answer to your question. You feel the pull because God is calling you. But you won't answer the call. When it is time to answer the call, it is between you and God. I, Angel, nor Destiny can answer for you. We can't stand beside you on the day of judgment. Angel and I will not stand next to one another as a married couple before God on judgment day. This is your walk with Him alone. We can talk with you, pray with you, share in wisdom, and disciple you. This is what He has called us to do. But your faith is supposed to be in Him and Him alone, not us and our teaching.

My brother, do you believe there is an afterlife? Do you believe there is a heaven and a hell?

DeVon: I don't know about that. But I do believe there is a God.

Jay: If you believe in one, you must believe in the other as well. The Bible warns us about the schemes of the enemy, that voice you've been hearing since you were younger. That is what is speaking to you. So just as you can hear him clearly, so can you hear the Father. It's all in what you feed. You feed the flesh, and the enemy will grow inside of you. After accepting Jesus as your Lord and Savior, you feed the spirit, and that is what will grow inside of you. They will most times be at war within you. But you will always win with the Holy Spirit. *Always*, brother. You must read the Bible for yourself. Not in hopes of getting the woman you love. But loving and accepting God and His will for your life so much that even if it cost you the woman you love, you can walk away for Christ. You must die to you so that you can live through Him.

DeVon: *(believing his brother and ready to surrender it all)* OK, man, what do I need to do? I want to try Him. It has to be better than this. This feels like death.

Jay: I am going to ask you a couple of questions. You just need to answer them honestly.

DeVon: OK

Jay: Do you confess that you are a sinner in need of a Savior?

DeVon: Yes

Jay: Because of Adam's sin in the garden, all men have been guilty and born into sin. You are not a sinner because you sin; you sin because you are a sinner. That is because Adam's penalty for sin fell upon all men of the earth that was to come. Therefore, you are born in sin and shaped in iniquity. Because of that sin, God the Father required a blood sacrifice to cover all sin. So, He sent His son Jesus to give His life and shed His blood for the remission of your sins, my sins, Destiny's, and Angel's. All our sins. We all have sinned and fallen short of the glory of God. Nothing else will satisfy your sin penalty but the shedding of Jesus's blood. And this, my brother, is the reason we need to be saved.

With that said, do you believe God sent His son Jesus to die on the cross for the remission of your sins? And that on the third day, He rose with all power in heaven and earth in His hand?

DeVon: Yes

Jay: Say this prayer with me. Dear Father, I believe that you are the son of God. And I believe that you died on the cross for my sins. I acknowledge that I am a sinner separated from you. Your Word says if I confess my sins, you are faithful and just to forgive me of my sins and that I shall be saved. [20] I thank you for hearing my prayer, and I receive you as my Lord and Savior, in Jesus' name. Amen.

DeVon: That's it?

Jay: That's it. Other than you confessed with your mouth. The final step is just simply a public announcement of your new life unto Christ Jesus by baptism.

DeVon: By what? What is that?

Jay: *(laughing as he realizes he has more discipling to do with DeVon than expected.)* I will talk with the pastor of my church and see if we can get you baptized. Meaning you will go down in the water and come up with a new creature in Christ. *Therefore, if any man be in Christ, he is a new creature. Old things are passed away, behold all things become new.* [21] Welcome to the body of Christ; you are now truly my brother!

---

20   1 John 1:9, KJV

21   2 Corinthians 5:17

The two men embraced each other in excitement. DeVon felt happy and at peace. He was excited. He felt hope for the first time since he could remember. He suddenly became nervous, and Jay could see it on his face.

Jay: What's wrong, man? You should be on cloud ten right now.

DeVon: I don't want you to leave. Whenever you guys leave, this feeling goes away.

Jay: My brother, that feeling you have is not from me. That is our Father's presence. He is with you always. He promises in His Word that He will never leave you nor forsake you. [22] Where is your Bible that she got you?

They walked into the kitchen, and he grabbed it and handed it to Jay. As Jay flipped through the pages and saw all the notes, he was blown away. DeVon realized that Jay was looking at the sticky notes Destiny had written.

DeVon: Yeah, she has all those little notes in there of Scriptures that she said really spoke to her spirit. She said it helped her to grow in faith of our Father.

Jay: This is beautiful, man. I tell you, beautiful. (*he closed the Bible and held it in his hand as he spoke to DeVon*). Look, man, I don't know. I can't tell you what God will do regarding the two of you being a couple. That is our Father's business. And if He is in your life and her life, that is all that matters. That the two of you individually are doing the work of your Father. He has a perfect plan for you. The only thing you need to be consumed with right now is this Word (*he held the Bible in the air*). Let this word feed you. Let it come to life in your heart, mind, and soul. If you eat of His Word and let it be the sword for the battles you will face, I promise this feeling you have will remain with you. Seek ye first the kingdom and His righteousness and

---

22   Hebrews 13:5, KJV

all things will be added to you. [23]

DeVon: You guys quote these Scriptures like they are written on the wall of your brain.

Jay: It is hidden in our hearts that no man should be able to take away the promises of God.

DeVon: I like that.

Jay: Alright, man, let me get out of here. I am tired. You stay keeping me in warfare. Jesus has gotten the victory, and tonight, He will allow me to rest.

DeVon did not fully understand, but it sounded good. He gave his brother another hug before he closed the door behind him. He went to the kitchen, grabbed the Bible, and decided he was going to hold on to this moment as long as possible. As he situated himself on the couch to read, he decided he would tell Destiny tomorrow, but tonight, it was just him and his Father and His words in this book. DeVon read until he fell asleep in the presence of the Lord.

The next day, he arose to a call from Jay letting him know that he had spoken with his pastor. He will be baptized on Sunday before the worship service. DeVon was excited. Six more days seemed too long, but God had waited on him for years. He can wait on the public announcement of his commitment to his Heavenly Father. Besides, he had come to enjoy his quiet time with Him.

Jay: Hey, man, have you told Destiny yet?

DeVon: Not yet. I just woke up. I was up reading half the night.

Jay: That is awesome, man. What were you reading?

DeVon: That armor of God that Paul talks about. I asked God to show me what He wanted me to read, and it led to Ephesians. I remembered you talking about it, so I was shocked. I felt in my heart that I needed this immediately, as hard as I was working for the enemy. He

---

23   Matthew 6:33

is coming back for me.

Jay: You are on to something. You know that feeling you felt. It is the Holy Spirit guiding you and speaking to you. Always be in sync with that voice because it is there to protect, keep, and guide you. I will let you go so you can get your day started. I will text you the address of the church. Feel free to invite Destiny to your baptism. We can all grab a bite to eat after church. This is a celebration, my brother.

DeVon was shocked by Jay and Angel's turn of feelings towards Destiny. However, he was thankful. It made the dynamics between all of them so much easier to deal with. DeVon felt weird that, for the first time, he was not consumed with being with her as much as he was consumed with his relationship with God now. It was just nice that everyone was getting along.

DeVon: Will do. And Jay, thank you. You and Angel have been heaven-sent. My brother, thank you for all you and your wife have done for me. I pray God blesses you both beyond what your mind can imagine.

Jay: You are welcome, and praise God for the things He has done.

The guys disconnected the call, and DeVon took a moment to talk with his Father and thank Him for the day. He then called Destiny and advised her of the good news. She was elated and, of course, accepted the invite to his baptism and celebration dinner. She didn't know what that meant for them, and truthfully, neither seemed to be concerned with that. She was thankful that another soul had been returned to God, and he was thankful to have been saved.

***

The night before the big day snuck up on DeVon fast. He had taken the last couple of days to put his house on the market, apply for an apartment, and submit his resume to several companies for employment. Next week, he would trade his car in for something more practical. Besides, the spirits that came with that car and house were of darkness, and he wanted nothing to do with them. DeVon had purposely missed several calls from his connect man, Kevo. But as he saw his name across his phone screen calling again, he realized he must face this matter and end it. He finally answered and informed Kevo that he would no longer need anything else. The last time was the last time.

Kevo: Run-Man, what's the problem? Haven't I been good to you?

DeVon: It's DeVon; I no longer acknowledge Run-Man, and he is no longer a part of my identity. I am saved now and will only respond to what my Heavenly Father calls me.

Run-Man: What? You didn't discuss this with me. What are you talking about, boy?

DeVon thought to himself, *and there he is*. Since he accepted Jesus Christ, he had been so into the Word and studying that he didn't hear that voice any longer. The minute he contacted someone in the world, his voice came alive. He was waiting for him.

While on the phone with Kevo and Run-Man, DeVon took the time to shut the enemy down with his sword, the word of God.

DeVon: "For we wrestle not against flesh and blood, but against principalities, against powers, against the rulers of the darkness of this world, against spiritual wickedness in high places." [24]

Father God, it is in this moment that the enemy speaks to me *(Run-Man's voice, sounding faint, says, "What?"),* and I recognize it is not of you because his conversation is not of your Word. I feel the darkness that has arrived. But you, my Father, are my light and my salvation in whom I trust. I pray, Lord God, that he will flee as I have resisted. I pray for the brother I am speaking with, and I ask you to search his heart, Lord God. If there be any recognition of you in a lost soul, I pray you call it forth in the name of Jesus. This is my prayer, Amen.

---

24   Ephesians 6:12

Ok, man, I said what I had to say. It's been…well, never mind. Be blessed, my brother, and one more thing. Call upon the name of the Lord, and He will save you.

With that last statement, DeVon disconnected the call and went on about his day. He decided it was a celebration, and he had nothing he would care to wear in the house of God. So, he headed to run a few errands. He called Destiny to see if she wanted to go with him. By the fall of the evening, they had gotten everything needed and that DeVon wanted for tomorrow. They even browsed a few furniture stores for his apartment because he decided he was selling the house with all furniture included.

DeVon pulled up to Destiny's house to drop her off. For the first time, he felt no need to do anything but walk her to the door. His mind was made up that if they decided to move forward with anything, God would have to grant them both permission, and they would do things "in order," as Destiny once said. Being in the house that she shared with her soon-to-be ex-husband was not in order. As they said their goodbyes, a familiar truck pulled into the driveway, and DeVon thought Satan himself had stepped out of the truck.

Chris: Well, well, well. What do we have here?

Destiny: Chris, what are you doing here?

DeVon said nothing but stood and witnessed the communication between a man and his soon-to-be ex-wife. As long as he was respectful, he would remain silent.

Chris: What do you mean, what am I doing here? This is my house, bit…

DeVon: Oh, wait, watch your mouth.

Chris: And if I don't?

Destiny: DeVon, baby, go home. I got this.

Chris: Baby? I knew it! I knew you were that…

DeVon: Again, man, watch your mouth. Let's not disrespect the lady.

Chris got in DeVon's face until they were nose and nose. Chris's fire was burning, and he was ready for war.

Chris: And who do you think you're talking to?

Run-Man: I'm talking to the coward I've been looking for.

Destiny heard a tone in his voice that she recognized immediately from the hospital.

Destiny: DeVon, what is going on?

Chris: Well, look no further.

Run-Man: Just what the doctor ordered. Let's take this one last dance.

Destiny: Father God, please help.

DeVon: *(realizing he is about to snap)* You know what, man? This is not what I am about to do. Baby, go in the house. I will call you later.

Run-Man: What, fool? You better get this, man!

DeVon: *(in his mind, he speaks to the spirit within)* I will call upon the name of the Lord. The armor, Lord; I need the word; bring a word to me.

Chris: Oh, look, y'all saved now. The two that destroyed my marriage, took my house, and changed my life now get to be saved together. How cute. I'm glad to know. I should have finished you off that night.

DeVon and Destiny both stood in shock, looking into the eyes of rage, anger, hostility, jealousy, hatred, ego, and pride. They both knew they were in trouble as Chris reached to his backside.

Chris: I tell you what, little lovers, let's make this date night. The two of you together get to go meet your maker, *together*!

Run-Man: (voice in DeVon's head sounding faint) Let me get him, DeVon. I got you, man. Remember, I showed you how to use your hands like a bullet.

DeVon grabbed Destiny's hand to pull her behind him and closed his eyes to pray God's weapon was stronger than the enemy. Run-Man knew that DeVon would freeze at this moment and had the same juice as the like-minded spirit he was looking at…

BOOM! They all heard what sounded like a bomb exploding in their ears…

To be Continued....

Author's Thoughts

In 2020, the world was faced with a global pandemic. Was it the first of its kind? No. However, it was the first time most of us had experienced such an event. Some people attempted to live life as if nothing had changed, even growing frustrated because of the inconvenience of living life as normal. Then, there were some of us who took a hard look at ourselves and our lives as they currently were, physically and spiritually. We didn't know if the world was coming to an end or if it was a thunderous sound of warning from heaven. One thing was for certain: no matter who you were and where you were in the entire world, you could not escape what was happening. I would imagine this is what the Rapture would look like, also.

While the world was on pause, I took a moment to reflect on my life. I thought that if I were to die, had I done everything I wanted to do? Or did I fall victim to a society that kept my mind focused on the things of the world—climbing the ladder of success in corporate America, obtaining the American dream of home ownership, and excursions of experiencing life on my own terms? I was moved by the very fact that my thought process at that moment was, "Did I do what I wanted?" In my silence, when no one else was around, and I was left alone with my thoughts, I considered the fact that throughout the years, I had not thought about God's assignment for my life. It was not at the forefront of my day-to-day thought process. I professed to be saved and knew Him. I even claimed to love Him. Yet my life reflected me, the flesh, and the sin I was born into. It reflected the shaping of my iniquities. My mind knew Him, and my heart thought of Him through the traditional acts of church service on Sunday and praying in times of need, but my spirit was His enemy. I was the very thing He despised. I was spiritually on life-support, and I was getting closer and closer to that one more dangerous decision that could have separated me from the love of God.

One Saturday, I was at a home décor store, going through the motions of life, thinking I was finally living right but still not sure what God thought about it. Perhaps I had done too much, and nothing I do now could change my destiny of destruction. As I stood in line at the register, waiting for my turn to check out, I saw two young men walk through the door. This shouldn't have bothered me, but it did. Everything within me said, "NOOOO" the moment I looked at them. As the elderly cashier motioned that it was my turn to check out, I heard two words that I would hold on to for the rest of my life: "MOVE NOW." It was undeniable, and if I wanted to ignore it, my being within wouldn't let me. I walked past the cashier, advising her that I was going to go grab something else. I'm not sure why I made that statement, but I moved instantly. Instead of leaving the store, I turned down the nearest aisle and stood there frozen. For a moment, I thought to myself, "Girl, you are losing your mind." A sudden scream pulled me back into reality. I wasn't losing my mind after all. The store was being robbed.

I ran alongside other customers to the back exit and out the door. Hiding alongside a couple behind a dumpster, my body shook as if I had no control of it. The husband decided if the robbers were to run, they would probably come to the back where we were. He found somewhere else to take his wife for safety. As they ran, I was left standing alone, crying and yelling to their backs, "Can I go with you? I'm by myself." Receiving no response, I ran in the opposite direction and into a grassy field as other customers ran also. Finally, I made it to my car. After catching my breath, I called my husband, who was at work. I was crying hysterically. He talked to me until I calmed down and was able to drive home. I sat on the couch sobbing in my fear of victimization when I was hit with a revelation. The obvious thought is I should have been thankful and praising God for that instant protection. For Him being an omnipresent Father who instructed the Holy Spirit to speak to me immediately. And while I am thankful for this, there was a bigger revelation. The true revelation was that I heard a voice, and that voice had to be the Holy Spirit warning me of danger. If the Holy Spirit was warning me of danger, it had to be because I belong to God. God the Father, the Son, and the Holy Spirit. After years of uncertainty, in seconds, He confirmed that not only was I His, but He would protect me. That He will never leave me nor forsake me.

It was at that moment that I realized I had another chance. I had another chance to be in this earth about my Father's business. I had another chance to build a relationship with Him. I had another chance to seek ye first the kingdom and His righteousness. I had another chance to try Him at His word with all my heart and all my soul. From that date to the present, I have served a 7-day-a-week, 365-day-a-year God. No more just Sunday morning service and one scripture to last me a week or two. I initially started with videos and clips of sermons daily, and that built my hunger, yet I still wasn't satisfied. He then sent one of His sons to disciple me and a friend. Without us realizing it, we were being discipled. His discipleship led me to read the Word for myself, the book written by those who walked the earth with His son Jesus and witnessed His healing power, His deliverance, and above all else, His death for our sins and His resurrection. Through His Word, I am satisfied. And continuously becoming satisfied. He is truly the living water, and in Him, I shall never thirst again.

My purpose for this book was to tell a realistic story because we live in a realistic, sinful world. We are deceived by the tricks of the enemy throughout everyday life, tricks that don't seem like sin at all. It's the planting of sinful seeds that have consumed our minds and grown in ways we couldn't imagine. While there are many sins we encounter, some are so hidden that they could blow your mind. Destiny was heartbroken and searching for someone to give her the love she longed for, the love she had seen on television since she was a child. Ask yourself, how could watching television be sinful? Easily, it can become the Lust of the Flesh, the Lust of the Eyes, and the Pride of life.

DeVon was also desiring love. With the death of his parent and grandmother, he felt lonely and just needed someone. Neither of them realized what they desired was understandable, but there was a thin line between desire and desperation. And if you are not careful, your decision to make it happen becomes dangerous. But God plants seeds in our lives as well, seeds that lead to the path of His glory. If you just take the time to pay attention, it is through the people around you, nature on a beautiful sunny or rainy day when the air is still, through the reading and studying of His Word, patience with yourself and others, love and forgiveness, understanding and compassion. He knows the desires of our hearts, and He also knows the plan He has for us. We must be more in tune with seeking Him and His plan than with our own desires.

I pray that when you have closed the last page of this book, you consider yourself and your relationship with the Father. Take inventory of your life, the time you make for work, family, and friends, cleaning up or planning for the coming days. Then, take inventory of the time you have set aside to build your relationship with the Father. Perhaps it's just me who realized I loved the thought of salvation. However, you spend time with those you love, and the truth is, I hadn't. If I am the only one, I am ok with that and hope you enjoyed the book. However, if anything pulled on the strings of your heart, and you recognize these thoughts in your own head and heart, don't beat yourself up like I did. Don't allow the enemy to torment you for years, keeping you wondering if you can be forgiven. As long as you have breath in your body, you have another chance. It is amazing that the time of right now is referred to as "the present." I believe it's because it is a gift. If you have breath right now, you have the gift of another chance. Let me pray with you.

Father God, in the name of Jesus, first, I want to say THANK YOU. Thank you for the gift of this moment. Thank you for being the creator of everything that is good and perfect. Thank you for being our creator. Father God, forgive us of our sins. Forgive us for taking time and the breath in our bodies for granted. Forgive us for making decisions that go against everything you have created us to be on this earth for your glory. Lord God, we repent of our sins, and we thank you for the blood of Jesus that was shed for the remission of our sins. Father, I pray that as I have lifted you up in this book, you will draw all readers unto you. I pray, Heavenly Father, that we will begin to hunger and thirst for you. I pray that you become our living water so that we shall never thirst again. I pray we become intentional in our time of prayer, reading, meditating, and worship and praise with you. I pray that you be to them what you have been to me, an omnipresent Father who has given me undeserved grace and mercy. Your love has kept me. You pursued me until I heard and responded to the call, and now I pursue you with love and hope of a future in you and with you. What wondrous love is this you have given, o my soul. You are HOLY. These blessings I pray for my family in you. I thank you for what you have done and, most of all, for what you will do in each of our lives. I will forever declare your name in the earth. It is in Jesus' name, I pray. Amen.

www.ingramcontent.com/pod-product-compliance
Lightning Source LLC
Chambersburg PA
CBHW071944190726
48293CB00004B/1337